# ROUGH
# WEATHER

# ROUGH WEATHER

## Robert B. Parker

**Doubleday Large Print
Home Library Edition**

**G. P. PUTNAM'S SONS
New York**

This Large Print Edition, prepared especially for Double-day Large Print Home Library, contains the complete, unabridged text of the original Publisher's Edition.

PUTNAM

G. P. PUTNAM'S SONS
**Publishers Since 1838**
Published by the Penguin Group
Penguin Group (USA) Inc., 375 Hudson Street,
New York, New York 10014, USA • Penguin Group
(Canada), 90 Eglinton Avenue East, Suite 700,
Toronto, Ontario M4P 2Y3, Canada (a division of
Pearson Canada Inc.) • Penguin Books Ltd,
80 Strand, London WC2R 0RL, England • Penguin
Ireland, 25 St Stephen's Green, Dublin 2, Ireland
(a division of Penguin Books Ltd) • Penguin Group
(Australia), 250 Camberwell Road, Camberwell,
Victoria 3124, Australia (a division of Pearson
Australia Group Pty Ltd) • Penguin Books India Pvt Ltd,
11 Community Centre, Panchsheel Park,
New Delhi–110 017, India • Penguin Group (NZ), 67
Apollo Drive, Rosedale, North Shore 0632,
New Zealand (a division of Pearson New Zealand
Ltd) • Penguin Books (South Africa) (Pty) Ltd,
24 Sturdee Avenue, Rosebank, Johannesburg 2196,
South Africa

Penguin Books Ltd, Registered Offices: 80 Strand, London WC2R 0RL, England

ISBN 978-1-60751-250-9

Printed in the United States of America

While the author has made every effort to provide accu-
rate telephone numbers and Internet addresses at the
time of publication, neither the publisher nor the author
assumes any responsibility for errors, or for changes
that occur after publication. Further, the publisher does
not have any control over and does not assume any
responsibility for author or third-party websites or their
content.

For Joan: the fact is the sweetest
dream of all.

# ROUGH WEATHER

# 1

*If I rolled my chair back* into the window bay behind my desk, I could look up past the office buildings and see the sky. It wasn't exactly overcast. It was kind of gray-ish, with the sun pushing weakly through the thin clouds. Below on Berkeley Street the young women from the insurance companies were starting to show fall fashions. I took some time to evaluate them, and concluded that fashionable dress was heavily dependent on who was wearing it. I looked at the calendar. September 13. Technically it was still baseball season, but the Sox had dropped out of contention at the beginning of August, leaving me with nothing else to think about but sex . . . which was, I thought, considerably better than the other way around.

I was thinking about sex when there was a delicate knock on my door. Immediately after the knock, the door opened and a woman came in for whom I was in the perfect frame of mind. She was a symphony of thick auburn hair, even features, wide mouth, big eyes, stunning figure, elegant clothes, expensive perfume, and what people who talked that way would call *breeding*. She came to my desk and put her hand out as I got to my feet.

"Hi," she said. "I'm Heidi."

I said, "I recognize you, Ms. Bradshaw."

She had a firm handshake, as if she had practiced.

"And you are Mr. Spenser," she said.

"Was it the name on the door, gave me away?" I said.

She nodded happily. And sat down in front of my desk and crossed her legs. *Wow!*

"I rather expected that it would," she said. "And you certainly look right for the part."

"Valiant?" I said.

"Valiant," she said. "And quite large."

"You ain't seen nothing yet," I said.

She looked at me for a moment and then said, "Really?"

I was too valiant to blush.

"In a manner of speaking," I said.

"I would like to hire you," she said.

"I was hoping," I said.

She smiled again and let the smile linger. Baseball traveled even further from my mind.

"I am a strong woman," she said. "Self-possessed, wealthy. I am also divorced, from someone who richly deserves it, and find myself occasionally insecure without a man."

"Anyone might," I said.

"Not necessarily," she said. "And I am working with my therapist to resolve that issue. In the meanwhile, I will indulge my insecurity if I must. I have a home on Tashtego Island. Do you know it?"

"The island, yes. The home, no."

"Aren't you precise," she said. "The home, too, is called Tashtego. My husband was a great fan of *Moby-Dick*. I am having an event there in late October, which will be attended by some of the most important and glamorous people in the world."

"And naturally, you want me to be one of them," I said.

She smiled that smile again. It was obvious that she knew what she could do with that smile.

"In a way," she said. "I would like to employ you as a kind of balance to my insecurity."

"An insecurity guard?"

"Exactly," she said. "I want you to be the man I can turn to if I need something."

"Will you want me to provide security in the more conventional sense as well?"

"No. The island has its own security patrol. You are there to support me."

"Unless your therapy kicks in before October," I said.

"Unless that," she said. "Or a whirlwind romance."

I nodded.

"May I bring a guest?"

"What kind of a guest?" she said.

"A stunning Jewess, with a Ph.D. from Harvard."

"Wife?"

"Not exactly," I said.

"Girlfriend?"

"Sort of," I said. "Think of her as The One."

"Why do you want to bring her?"

"I miss her when I'm not with her," I said. "And it'll make me feel less like a gigolo."

She laughed out loud.

"You're so cute," she said. "Of course, bring The One."

"Would you like to talk costs?" I said.

She took a green leather checkbook out of her purse.

"Not very much," she said. "May I pay you a large retainer?"

"Good start," I said.

# 2

*I was having dinner* with The One at a new place called Sorellina.

"You know, of course, who Heidi Bradshaw is," Susan said.

"My client."

"Besides that," Susan said.

"She's famous," I said.

"Do you know for what?"

"Besides being my client?" I said.

"Besides that," Susan said.

"I guess she's famous for being famous," I said.

The room was large and not loud. The tables were well spaced. There were windows where you could look out at Copley Square. The service was good. I was paying with a small part of Heidi Bradshaw's swell advance. . . . And I was with the girl of my dreams.

"She has been married to some of the richest men in the world," Susan said.

"And profited from each marriage," I said.

"Any girl would," Susan said. "How did she find you."

"Maybe she Googled *stud* on the Internet?"

"I've tried that," Susan said. "You're not listed."

"Damn," I said.

"So, how did they end up with you?"

"Somebody called somebody," I said. "And one thing led to another?"

"Okay, and if it worked that way, what would be the basis for recommending you?"

"I'm a great husband substitute?" I said.

"Probably not," Susan said.

"That I'm a tough guy, and I own a gun?" I said.

"Probably so," Susan said.

We were quiet for a moment. Susan had

some sort of exotic fish. She took a small bite. Susan always took small bites. She ate slowly, and rarely ate all of what she ordered. I had pasta, all of which I guzzled.

"I thought of that," I said.

"Me, too," Susan said.

"So why do you hire a guy with a gun to hang around your party?"

"Because you're afraid," Susan said.

"Even though the island has its own security."

"Even though," Susan said.

"Maybe you're afraid of the security," I said.

"Maybe she thinks they're incompetent."

"For crissake," I said. "It's her island. They are her security."

Susan shrugged and nibbled on her fish. I finished the last meatball. Susan took a small sip of wine.

"Well, whatever the reason," she said. "She feels the need to augment it."

"With one guy?"

"Apparently," Susan said. "Which is why the one guy is you."

"Shucks," I said.

"Which means they went looking for you," Susan said. "Or someone like you."

"Which means maybe I should bring two guns?"

"One should be enough," Susan said. "You are, after all, bringing me."

# 3

*Tashtego Island* had its own ferry service, a high-speed catamaran that shuttled people to and from the island every day. The trip took about forty minutes from New Bedford. The island rose like a single black rock from Buzzards Bay, and the house gleamed on top of it. White marble among the hardy trees softened the hardness of the stone.

"I think I hear the theme from *Camelot,*" Susan said.

She had brought enough luggage for the weekend to sustain Cirque du Soleil. But the number of servants meeting the boat

was more than sufficient to the task, and I
walked ashore unencumbered. There was
a small dock house made of the same
white stone as the big house. Parked beside the dock house was a white Jeep. In
the white Jeep were two guys in safari jack-
ets, wearing aviator glasses and carrying
sidearms in polished cordovan-leather holsters. In front of the dock house was an
open carriage. The two big horses in har-
ness were white. The driver had a blond
crew cut. He wore a blazer and white
slacks, and looked like a big college kid.
Maybe a middle linebacker. I patted one of
the horses on the flank.

"Clydesdales?" I said.

"Belgians," he said. "In medieval times
they were warhorses."

"Big," I said.

"Yes, sir."

Beside the carriage was a square-jawed
woman in a mannish-looking white shirt
and gray flannel slacks. There was a cell
phone on her belt. She was too old for
college by now, and she wasn't actually
so big, but there was a hint of linebacker
about her, too. I wondered if Smith had a
team.

"Mr. Spenser," she said. "I'm Maggie Lane, Mrs. Bradshaw's assistant."

We shook hands. I introduced Susan. They shook hands. One of the horses looked over his shoulder at us without interest. Maggie Lane gestured toward the carriage.

"Please," she said.

"Luggage?" Susan said.

"It will be delivered to your rooms," Maggie Lane said.

For Susan, the thought that her luggage was in alien hands was nearly life-threatening. But she simply smiled and got into the carriage. Her clothes fit her well, and I admired her agility as she stepped up into the carriage. Also her backside. I followed, and Maggie Lane stepped up beside the driver.

"Except for the patrol Jeeps," she said, "there are no cars on the island."

"How lovely for the ambience," Susan said.

"And the atmosphere," Maggie Lane said.

"Good source of fertilizer, too," I said.

Maggie Lane nodded with a smile, though I didn't think the smile was terribly warm. The ride from the dock wasn't steep enough to bother the big Belgians, that I could tell. It wound slowly around the rising rock, with the ocean on our right and the south coast of Massachusetts still visible on the horizon behind us, until we leveled out on the flat top of the rock where the house was, surrounded by trees and gardens, beneficiaries, no doubt, of the horses' largesse. Such greenery hadn't settled on top of this rock by accident, and it had not exfoliated so richly without help.

The house itself looked like it had been constructed by Cornelius Vanderbilt. It looked like someplace you could catch a sleeper train for Chicago. There were columns and friezes and arched windows twenty feet high.

"We have a small suite for you in the northeast corner of the house," Maggie Lane said. "Not far from Mrs. Bradshaw's private quarters."

I sort of thought everyone's quarters were private but decided not to raise the question.

"And the luggage?" Susan said.

"It should be there waiting for you,"

Maggie Lane said. "Unpacked, and carefully hung up."

Susan blanched slightly. But Maggie Lane was looking toward the house and didn't notice. I knew that the thought of anyone opening Susan's luggage and carefully hanging up her stuff was unbearable.

With her lips barely parted she said, "Oh, how lovely."

The crushed-shell driveway gleaming white in the morning sun curved in front of the vast marble pile of a house and under a two-story porte cochere. Another young guy in a blazer and white pants, maybe an outside linebacker, came to help us from the carriage. Susan hated that. She jumped down briskly before he was able to get there. I dismounted more sedately but no less athletically. In front of us, and closer to the house, was another white Jeep with two guys in it wearing safari shirts and sunglasses and gun belts. Like the two guys at the dock, they had inconspicuous earpieces.

Maggie Lane took us in through a front door that could accommodate a family of giraffes. We stood in a foyer that would have accommodated the Serengeti Plain, at the foot of a vast curving staircase that probably went to heaven.

"Stay close," I murmured to Susan.

We went past the staircase and down the corridor, which narrowed to maybe thirty feet behind the stairs. There was a pair of huge French doors at the far end, and the light poured in happily. On the wall were well-framed oil paintings of people who were almost certainly rich, and pleased about it. Halfway down the corridor, Maggie Lane stopped, took out some keys, and opened a door on the left.

"Here we are," she said, and handed me two keys. "I'll let you freshen up a little."

She took a card from the pocket of her shirt.

"Everything should be provided for," she said. "But if you need anything you don't have, anything at all, call me and I'll make it happen. The butler will be by to take your lunch order."

I took the card. We went in. Maggie Lane closed the door behind us. We stood and looked at each other for a moment, then we explored. It took a while. It is not inaccurate to say simply that there was a living room, two bedrooms, two baths, and a kitchenette. It is also not inaccurate to say that Niagara is a waterfall. The living room was a sufficient size for basketball. A polished mahogany bar divided the living room from the kitchenette. A hall with a black-and-brown tiled floor led to a couple of bedrooms, each with its own bath. The wall of arched windows opposite the door gave us a twenty-foot-high view of the sloping lawn behind the house and, past that, of the Atlantic Ocean stretching toward Europe. The room itself was sand-colored: walls, ceiling, rugs, sofas, upholstered chairs. The wood was mahogany. The accent colors were mahogany and black.

We looked around for a while in perfect silence. When we got back to the living room, Susan turned to me.

"Sweet Jesus," she said.

# 4

*Lunch was lobster and mango salad* with fresh rolls and a bottle of white Grave. Susan and I put the wine away for later. After lunch we toured the grounds, which were everything that grounds ought to be. It was a warm and pleasant day for October. We found a bench near the front of the house and sat on it and watched the guests begin to gather.

"Exactly what is this event," Susan said. "You've never said."

"You never asked."

"I was just so thrilled you invited me," Susan said. "I was nearly speechless."

"Understandable," I said. "The central

event is the marriage of Heidi Bradshaw's daughter, Adelaide, to a guy named Maurice Lessard, whose family owns a pharmaceutical company."

"Adelaide?" Susan said.

"Ever-loving Adelaide," I said.

"How old?" Susan said.

"Twenty-two, I think."

"Puts Heidi in her forties, then," Susan said.

"I'd guess," I said.

Heidi Bradshaw came across the lawn at full stride.

"I'm so, so sorry," she said, "not to have been here to greet you when you arrived."

"Busy time," I said, and introduced Susan.

"I'm thrilled, Miss Silverman," Heidi said. "I've heard the big boy here speak very well of you."

"My pleasure," Susan said.

Susan was perfectly pleasant, but I could hear the chill.

"Actually," I said. "It's Dr. Silverman."

"Really?" Heidi said to Susan. "A medical doctor."

"I'm a psychotherapist," Susan said. "But please, call me Susan."

"Therapist? How fascinating. Is it fun?"

"Not always," Susan said.

"Well, I bet it's useful for managing the stud, here," Heidi said, and shared an intimate smile with me.

"Sadly, I'm not trained in adolescent psychology," Susan said.

"Oh, you're so funny," Heidi said. "Omigod, there's Leopold."

She turned from us and rushed into the arms of a darkly tanned gentleman with white hair, who might have been a famous conductor, as he was stepping from the carriage.

"Did we find her annoying?" I said to Susan.

"We did."

"Was it the 'Miss Silverman' that did it?" I said.

"You seemed quick to correct her," Susan said.

"I felt your pain," I said.

"It was a put-down."

"To call you 'Miss'?"

"Trust me," Susan said. "And she was so intimately proprietary with you."

"Intimately?" I said.

Susan said, "Yes . . . stud boy."

"I don't know how it looks for us in the long term, though," I said. "She dropped me for that orchestra leader in a millisecond."

"I don't like her," Susan said.

I was looking at her. She was looking at the people climbing out of the second carriage. Her face stiffened.

"Oh my good God," she said.

I looked. Stepping out of the carriage, dressed as usual, and carrying a small suitcase, was the Gray Man. He glanced over at us. I looked back. He gave no sign.

"Friend of the bride?" I said to Susan. "Or friend of the groom?"

# 5

*"Maybe he doesn't see us,"* Susan said.

"He sees us."

"How can you be sure?"

"Rugar doesn't not see things," I said.

"Is that really his name, do you think?"

"It's the one he used last time," I said.

"In Marshport?"

"Yeah," I said, "two, three years ago."

"When he helped you?"

"Yep."

"How about when he almost killed you?"

"Yeah, he was Rugar then, too," I said. "Almost ten years."

Carrying his small suitcase, Rugar walked across the lawn toward us.

"Dr. Silverman," he said to Susan. "A pleasure to see you again."

Susan nodded without saying anything. Rugar was wearing a gray blazer, gray slacks, a gray shirt with a Windsor collar and sapphire cuff links, a charcoal tie with a sapphire tie clasp, and black shoes with pointy toes.

"Spenser," Rugar said.

"Rugar," I said.

He smiled.

"Our paths seem to keep crossing," Rugar said.

"Kismet," I said.

"I hope we are not here on conflicting missions," Rugar said.

"Tell me what you're here for," I said, "and I can tell you if there's conflict."

Rugar smiled again. It was more of an automatic facial gesture than an expression of anything.

"You could," Rugar said. "But you wouldn't."

"How do you know?" I said.

"Because I wouldn't," Rugar said.

"I'm not sure we're as much alike as you think we are," I said.

"We seemed rather alike in Marshport," Rugar said.

"The first time we met, you almost killed me," I said.

"But I didn't," Rugar said. "You almost put me in jail."

"But I didn't," I said.

"So I guess we are starting even here," Rugar said.

"You wish," I said.

Again, the meaningless smile.

"You have never lacked for confidence," he said.

"Never had reason to," I said.

"And perhaps you are more playful than I," Rugar said.

"There are viruses more playful than you are," I said.

Rugar nodded.

"But you know as well as I do," he said, "that the game we play has neither winners nor losers. There are only the quick and the dead."

"I know that," I said.

"Makes the game worth playing, perhaps."

"Especially for the quick," I said.

"'Only when love and need are one . . .'" Rugar said.

"'And the work is play for mortal stakes . . .'?"

"You know the verse," Rugar said.

"You assumed I would," I said.

"I did," Rugar said.

"We quick are a literate bunch."

"Let us hope it continues," Rugar said.

He nodded gravely to Susan.

"Perhaps we'll chat again," he said.

We watched him walk back across the lawn toward the house. Susan hugged herself.

"God," Susan said. "It's as if there's a chill where he's been."

"If I remember right, at the depths of Dante's Inferno," I said, "Satan is frozen in ice."

"It's as if Rugar has no soul," Susan said.

"Probably doesn't," I said. "Got a couple of rules, I think. But soul is open to question."

"Does he frighten you?"

"Probably," I said. "If I think about it. He's pretty frightful."

"But . . . that won't influence what you do," she said.

"No."

The day had darkened. I looked up. Clouds had begun to gather between us and the sun. The day was still. There was no wind at all.

"Gee," I said. "He really does leave a chill."

Susan glanced up at the sky and shrugged slightly. When she was focused on something, it was hard to get her off it.

"Do you think it's a coincidence that he's here and you're here?" Susan said.

"Hard to figure how it wouldn't be," I said.

"But do you think it is?" Susan said.

"No. I don't think it's a coincidence."

"So if it isn't," Susan said, "what does it mean?"

"I don't know," I said.

"So you'll just plow along," Susan said, "doing what you do, and awaiting developments."

"Yuh," I said.

# 6

*By the time I had mastered* my tuxedo and clipped on my bow tie (fashion titan though I was, I had never accomplished the art of the bow tie), the view through the tall windows was gray. The skies were dark and low. The ocean was nearly the same color and very still. It took a long stare to see the line where the horizon traced between them. There was still no wind, but there was something in the atmosphere that suggested that some wind would be along.

I had a foot up on an ivory-colored hassock and was putting a short .38 revolver

into an ankle holster when Susan came
down the hall in a white dress that fit her
well. She looked like she was receiving
an Academy Award for stunningness. I took
my foot off the hassock and put it on the
floor and shook the pant leg down over
the gun.

"Wow!" I said.

She smiled.

"I thought much the same thing when I
looked in the mirror," she said.

"How about me?" I said.

"I thought you'd say 'Wow!' too," she
said.

"No, my appearance," I said. "Don't I remind you of Cary Grant?"

"Very much," Susan said, "except for
looking good."

"That's not the way you were talking an
hour ago," I said.

"An hour ago," Susan said, "you were
seducing me."

"Which wasn't that difficult," I said.

"No," she said. "It wasn't."

We stood together, looking out at the
gathering weather.

"I thought the storm was supposed to
miss us," Susan said.

"You can't believe the weather weenies," I said.

"What's left," Susan said.

"Don't get existential on me," I said.

She smiled and looked at me carefully.

"You seem so unlikely a person to own his own tux," Susan said.

"It's hard to find my size in the rental stores," I said.

"Or anywhere else, I would imagine," Susan said. "Did you tie that bow tie?"

"I don't know how," I said. "If I bought one, could you tie it for me?"

"I don't know how," Susan said.

"The things you do know," I said, "more than compensate."

"Well, no one can tell if it's a clip-on anyway," she said.

We looked out the window some more.

"What is the plan?" Susan said.

"We meet in the chapel," I said, "at four. We stay with Heidi Bradshaw, sitting in her pew during the ceremony and being handy during the reception."

"The chapel," Susan said.

"I think on other days it's a library," I said. "But Heidi's party planner has chapel-ized it for today."

Far out to sea, a vertical flash of lightning appeared fleetingly.

"Don't see that so much," I said. "This time of year."

Susan nodded. Her shoulder pressed against my upper arm as we stood. There was a kind of breathlessness in the air outside the window, as if the lightning had ratcheted up the tension in the atmosphere.

"Why do you think he's here?" Susan said.

I knew who she meant.

"He's not a social kind of guy," I said. "I assume it's business."

She nodded.

"We don't really know quite why you're here," she said.

"Same answer," I said.

"Maybe he doesn't know, either," Susan said.

"Maybe," I said.

The lightning flashed again, and the leaves on some of the trees near the house had begun trembling faintly. Susan turned suddenly against me and put her arms around me and pressed her face against my chest. It was almost unthinkable that she would hug me at such a time and mess up her outfit. I put my arms around her lightly and patted her softly.

"If he kills you," she said, quite calmly, "I will die."

"That would make two of us," I said. "He won't kill me."

"I would die," Susan said.

The first scatter of raindrops hit the window.

"No one's done it yet," I said.

"He came close ten years ago," Susan said.

"Close only counts in horseshoes," I said.

I patted her gently on the backside. She nodded and straightened.

"You can't leave this alone," she said. "Can you?"

"No," I said.

"I understand," she said.

"I know you do."

"It was the gun," she said. "Seeing you put on the gun."

"I always wear a gun," I said.

"I know."

"We need to get going," I said.

"Yes," she said.

We stood for a bit longer with our arms around each other, while the rain became more frequent against the big window. Then Susan stepped back and looked at me and smiled.

"Here we go," she said. "Let me just check the mirror that having a mini-breakdown hasn't messed up my look."

"Nothing could," I said.

She walked to a full-length mirror at the end of the hall and studied herself for a moment.

"You know?" she said. "You're right."

# 7

*As we walked the long corridor* toward the chapel, I could hear the faint sound of a helicopter landing on the pad behind the house on the south side of the island. A helicopter is like a tank. Once you've heard one, you always remember.

"Late," I said to Susan.

"What?"

"Chopper," I said. "Lucky they got down before the storm starts to rumba."

"You think the storm will get worse?"

"Yes."

"I didn't even hear the helicopter," Susan said.

"That's because you're focused on me in my tux," I said.

"Of course," she said. "You're always listening, aren't you?"

I nodded.

"Sometimes I peek," I said.

She looked at me sideways as we walked.

"I'm aware of that," she said.

Behind us, lightning spilled briefly into the hall through the big French doors. A few seconds later there was a grumble of thunder.

"Storm's still a ways off," I said.

"Something about the time between the lightning and the thunder?" Susan said.

"Lightning's traveling at the speed of light," I said. "Thunder's coming at the speed of sound. The closer they are, the more they coincide."

"My God, Holmes," Susan said in her lowest voice. "Is there no limit to your knowledge?"

"I've never quite been able to answer, 'What does a woman want?'"

Susan smiled and banged my shoulder lightly with her head. In a small anteroom to the former library, Heidi and her daughter stood with Maggie Lane. With them was the famous conductor with the tan and the silver hair. Heidi was in her imperious mode. She introduced us quite formally. Actually, she introduced me, and I introduced Susan. Did Susan not notice? . . . Fat chance!

Adelaide was in full wedding dress, except there was no train. Probably couldn't find train carriers. She had a small face, which looked even smaller because she had so much red hair insufficiently contained by her veil.

"Adelaide's father chose not to attend," Heidi said. "Leopold will be taking Adelaide down the aisle."

"Okay," I said.

"You'll wait here with us, Mr. Spenser," Heidi said. "Dr. Silverman, an usher will take you to the first row on the right. Mr. Spenser will join you. Please sit at the far end, near the wall."

"Okay," I said.

I was in my docile mode. Susan winked at me and followed the usher out of the anteroom. Through the window behind me, lightning flashed again. And not very long after, the thunder grumbled. No one paid any attention.

"You'll be the last to enter the room, Mr. Spenser, after Leopold has delivered Adelaide to her husband. Please try to be unobtrusive."

"On little cat's feet," I said.

I doubt that Heidi even heard me.

"Mo-th-er," Adelaide said, making it into several syllables. "Everyone's here. It's time to start."

Heidi was nodding absently. The anteroom door had a small peephole in it that allowed you to see into the chapel. Heidi appeared to be counting the house.

"Why does the library door have a peephole?" I said. "Keep people from stealing the books?"

"When it was built it was thought to add a secretive medieval quality," Maggie Lane said.

I nodded. I could hear the string ensemble playing appropriate music as the guests were escorted in.

After a time, Heidi said, "All right, I'll go."

She looked at her daughter.

"Let me get seated before you and Leopold begin," Heidi said. "Just like we rehearsed. Maggie, don't let them start too soon."

"Mo-th-er . . ." Adelaide said.

Heidi smiled and stepped away from the peephole. Heidi leaned forward and kissed her daughter, carefully, no messing up the look.

"It'll be perfect," she said to Adelaide.

She put her hand on Adelaide's cheek for a moment. Then she turned and went out the other anteroom door into the hall. I took her place peeking through the door, and watched her appear a moment later at the double doors to the chapel. She came down the aisle alone, the mother of the bride, like a queen at her coronation. She was erect, beautiful, elegantly dressed, and perfectly done, with just the right amount of hip swing. I felt sort of bad for the anticlimactic Adelaide.

Maggie wanted to peek, too, and I sensed her resentment. But my docile mode took me only so far. After Heidi's long promenade, she slipped into her seat in the first pew. I could almost feel the impulse to applaud run through the chapel, but everyone fought it off successfully.

"Okay," I said.

"Okay," Maggie said, as if trying to void any usurpation of her position.

Leopold put his arm out. Adelaide, looking pallid and swallowing often, put her hand on his arm. He patted it and they went out of the anteroom. I followed them discreetly. They went through the big entrance to the chapel. The musicians, cued from the anteroom, I assumed, by the grim and ubiquitous Maggie, began to play "Here Comes the Bride." Leopold and Adelaide started down the aisle toward the waiting groom. Adelaide seemed pulled in upon herself, smaller than her mother, somehow frail-looking, as if the support of Leopold's arm was more than symbolic. After they got to the waiting groom and Leopold had retired to his pew, I skirted the back row more silently than the yellow fog, and went down along the side and sat where I'd been told.

# 8

*It may have begun* the day as a library, and it might be a library tomorrow, but at this moment it was every inch a chapel. The ceiling had been draped in dark gauze so that it seemed to reach a peak. The seating was in real pews, not folding chairs. There were hymnals in each pew. A small program lay on the seat in each place. The bookcases were draped in the same dark gauze they'd hung from the ceiling, and stained-glass windows hung in place. The lighting was provided by candles. In front was an altar of ornately carved wood that looked as if it had been lifted from a medieval church in Nottingham. There were flowers everywhere, huge vases as tall as I was, standing in exactly the right places, hanging flowers, flowers smothering the altar.

In the back-left corner of the room a string trio supplied the music. Around the room were people I recognized. A famous movie couple, an actor from New York, a tennis player, two senators. A lot of the women were good-looking; money always seems to help in that area. Everyone was dressed to the teeth. Like me. A hint of expensive perfume, nearly extinguished by the smell of the flowers, drifted through the room. I did not see the Gray Man. Susan was looking through the program.

"Bride's name is Van Meer," Susan whispered. "Her father must be the second husband, Peter Van Meer."

I nodded.

"Do I look better in my tux than the groom?" I whispered to Susan.

"No," she whispered back.

"Do too," I whispered.

Susan put her finger to her lips and nodded toward the altar. The minister was there in full high-church regalia, holding a prayer book open in his hands. He began the familiar recitation.

"Dearly beloved . . ."

The room was windowless for the wedding. But through the muffling gauze, and over the minister's orotund voice, I heard the crack of thunder. Some people in the chapel jumped slightly at the sound. The storm was very close. In fact, it might have arrived. But it was remote from the ceremony, shielded as we were by walls and curtains, gauze, and wealth. The ceremony proceeded just as if there were no storm.

". . . you may kiss the bride," the minister said.

They kissed. Neither husband nor wife seemed terribly enthusiastic about it. There was a slight rustle of movement at the back. Someone had arrived, quite probably by helicopter. Six men came in, wearing wet raincoats. Three went left and three went right.

And as they spread out, Rugar appeared with no coat, his gray suit perfectly dry except for the cuffs of his pants. His shoes were wet. They squished faintly as he began to walk down the center aisle toward the bride and groom. The six men took automatic weapons from under their raincoats. I had an impulse toward my ankle holster and realized it was a bad idea in a room crowded with wedding guests, and six guys with MP9s. The minister hadn't noticed the submachine guns yet. He was looking at Rugar with contained annoyance.

"Excuse me, sir," the minister said to Rugar, "but I would prefer . . ."

Rugar took out a handgun, it looked like a Glock, and shot the minister in the center of the forehead. The minister fell backward onto the floor in front of the altar. He convulsed a little and then lay still. Rugar turned toward the congregation, holding the Glock comfortably at his side. He was wearing a beautifully cut gray suit, a gray shirt, and a silver silk tie.

"Everyone is to stay calm and sit perfectly still," he said.

He looked at me, as if he knew right where I'd be.

"Particularly," he said, "you."

I nodded slightly. How flattering to be singled out.

"Anyone who interferes with me will be killed," Rugar said. "Anyone attempting to leave this room in the next hour will be killed. If I find you annoying, you will be killed."

The silence in the room was nearly impenetrable. Rugar took the bride's arm.

"Come along," he said.

She looked at her mother. Her mother was rigid. The groom was very pale. I could see him trying to get his breath. *Don't do it, kid. It won't help her. It'll get you killed.* He was too young. He'd seen too many movies, where heroism is required and the hero doesn't get killed.

"You can't do this," he said.

Rugar smiled almost sadly and shook his head almost sadly, and put his gun against the bridge of the kid's nose and pulled the trigger. It blew the back of his head out, and there was a lot of blood and brains. A soft sigh ran through the room as he went down. Adelaide stared for a moment, then fainted. Rugar broke her fall easily and let her slide to the floor. He looked without expression around the chapel.

"Anyone else?" he said.

No one spoke. I could feel the tension in Susan as her shoulder pressed against mine. Rugar looked down at Adelaide.

"Spenser," he said. "You're big and strong. You carry her."

Susan put her hand on my thigh.

"I've got a roomful of hostages," Rugar said. "I could kill some."

Susan patted my thigh and took her hand away.

"I'll carry her," I said.

# 9

*Whatever Rugar had worn* as a raincoat coming to the chapel, he didn't bother with on the way out. He stopped before we went out of the building and looked at me.

"You understand about the hostages," he said.

"I do."

"That would include Dr. Silverman."

"I understand that," I said.

We went bareheaded and without rainwear out into the tempest. One of the gunmen came with us, walking two steps behind me with his MP9 pointing at my back, his shoulders hunched, squinting through the assault of the rain. The tempest was startling. The rain was almost horizontal, driven by what must have been hurricane-level winds. I had Adelaide over my shoulder like a sack of wheat. She seemed to have re-achieved a small level of consciousness but no strength. She was as limp as an overcooked bean sprout. The rain soaked all three of us almost instantly. With Adelaide adding to my wind resistance, it was hard to be agile. Rugar walked through it, bent forward slightly, without looking back at me. It was very dark. I realized suddenly that there were no lights on in the big house. I looked back at the chapel wing. I could see no lights there. The electrical power must have succumbed to the storm.

Lightning flashed. Ahead of us there was something in the darkness. We had to get right next to it before I could be sure it was the helicopter. It was a big one. I knew little of recent helicopters, but this one was clearly capable of lifting at least a platoon of evildoers. Rugar opened a side door of the helicopter.

"Strap her in the seat," he said. "Here."

The pilot appeared with a big flashlight

and held it while I maneuvered Adelaide into a seat along the side of the chopper and buckled her in. Her eyes were open, but she still looked as if without the seat belt she'd collapse.

Rugar turned to the pilot.

"Can you fly in this weather?" he said.

"Oh my good God, no," the pilot said. "We can't get up until the storm passes."

"And if I order you?"

"Order away," the pilot said. "Even if we wanted to die, we can't get off the ground." He spoke like a native-born American, though not from the Northeast, but in the ambient light from the helicopter instrument panel I could see he was Asian. Japanese, probably. He wore a leather jacket unzipped, and a baseball hat. I could see the butt of a gun in a shoulder holster.

"Will the vehicle survive on the ground?" Rugar said.

"You mean will the hurricane blow it over?" the pilot said. "No, it's big and heavy and low and aerodynamic. It should stay put."

"How long?"

"Morning," the pilot said. "In the morning it'll be beautiful."

"How about a boat?" Rugar said.

"I don't do boats," the pilot said. "But I'll guarantee you that any boat on the island will swamp ten feet out from the dock, if they haven't torn lose and blown away already."

Rugar nodded. He looked at me.

"I'll accept your surrender," I said.

He almost smiled, but didn't answer me.

"We can't get out," he said. "But no one can get in."

"What are we gonna do?" the guy with the MP9 said.

"I'll let you know," Rugar said. "Take him back to the wedding and wait."

"Hold them there?"

"Yes."

The gunny and I turned back toward the house. Five feet from the helicopter I couldn't see it. The wind was blowing at my back now, making it hard not to fall forward.

"We're going the wrong way," I said to the gunny.

"Keep going," he said.

I turned a little so that the drenching wind slanted more at me from the side.

"You want to wander around in this all

night?" I said. "We're going away from the house."

"Keep moving," he said, but he turned the way I had.

I did the small maneuver a couple more times, until the rain was driving like buckshot straight into our faces.

"It was like this walking out here," the gunny said, trying to see me through the pelting tempest.

"The wind has shifted, you idiot," I said. "It always does in a hurricane."

If I was right, we were near the water's edge, on the back side of a big stone barn. We moved on. The wind was heavier. The rain more dense. I could feel, more than I could see, the barn on my left, and we hunched against it as we moved along. It didn't do much to shelter us. The wind and rain were howling along its side directly at us. I knew the far end of the barn was maybe thirty feet from the cliffs. Lightning blared for a moment. I was right. It was there, and forty or fifty feet below was the ocean. When we reached the far end, barely able to see, I stepped suddenly to the left, around the corner of the barn, and sprinted.

"You sonova bitch," I heard the gunny

say, and heard his footsteps. I was far enough from him in the howling murk that I knew he couldn't see me. I turned the next corner and flattened against the wall. When he came around after me, I lunged into him with my right shoulder. It staggered him, and his gun went flying. I brought my right forearm around and caught him on the side of his face. He got his arms around me and buried his cheek into my shoulder so it was hard to hit him, and both of us went down in the slick mud. It was like wrestling in deep oil sludge. He tried to get his knee into my groin and I twisted my hip so he couldn't. I got hold of his hair and pulled his head out away from my shoulder. We rolled over in the muck. I banged his nose with my forehead. He let go of me and got his hands on my throat. I head-butted him again. He tried to choke me. I bit his forearm. He grunted but kept choking. I gave him another head-butt. He didn't let go. I freed my left hand from under him and put my forearm against his throat and pushed his head up, pulling it back farther with my right hand in his hair. Suddenly he let go of my throat and tried to pull my forearm away. I kept the pressure. He rolled over beneath me. It was too slippery to stop him. I tried to get my forearm back under his neck but he wriggled away, and then we were on our feet again, wading through the saturated soil in mud past our ankles. I went after him as best I could. I think he wanted to run. But he wasn't sure what direction. He tried to feint left, like a punt returner, and go right. But in the swamp we were in, footwork was primitive. He slid a little and I was on him, trying to keep my feet under me. Neither of us had enough footing to land a decent punch. Then he made a mistake. He tried to kick me and lost his footing and staggered to his left. I turned my hip in a little and hit him with a big uppercut. Bingo! He staggered. I hit him again and he disappeared. I stared. I hadn't knocked him down. He was gone. I dropped to my hands and knees and crawled forward, feeling ahead of me. Where was the lightning when I needed it? I felt the cliff edge. I had, in fact, knocked him down. A lot farther down than I had imagined.

I inched forward slightly and looked down. Nothing but darkness. I listened. Nothing but storm. I inched back from the cliff and stood and walked to the barn, and sat down suddenly and without intending to, with my back on the barn wall and gasping. I was plastered with mud and grass. My tuxedo was infinitely wet. I'd have to get out of it before it dried, or it would probably strangle me. Though my clothes drying was not an immediate issue.

The immediate issue was to get Susan out of there. If I got her safe, I could begin to do something about the other problems. But until she was safe there were no other problems.

There was only Susan.

# 10

*After a time* I got enough oxygen in to stand up. The swarming rain had washed off some of the muck but not enough. I looked around a little for the MP9 that had been lost in the fight, but I couldn't find it in the blackness, and I was very aware of the nearby precipice. Firepower was probably not the right approach anyway. Against at least six guys with automatic weapons, guile seemed the better strategy.

I shrugged out of my waterlogged tuxedo jacket. My nice clip-on bow tie and several shirt studs had disappeared during the fight. I left the coat by the barn and began to push my way through the hurricane back toward the chapel. If Rugar went back there before I did, he would know that something was amiss. There was nothing I could do about that. It would make him very alert about Susan. He wouldn't kill her. He'd know that she was a valuable commodity in dealing with me. If he was there before me, she was safe as long as I was alive and on the loose.

I moved on, pressing against the palpable resistance of the storm. It was time now to stop feeling. Now I could do no one any good if I worked off of fear or rage or the frantic pressure to know that Susan was okay. Now I needed to put that away. Now, to rescue Susan, I would need to stop thinking of her. Now it was me and Rugar and no time for anything else.

It was a little hard to plan ahead, since I didn't know where Rugar was, or what was waiting back at the chapel. My guess was that Rugar would hold everyone hostage until the storm let up enough for him to get off the island. Even if some intrepid soul with a cell phone had alerted the cops on the mainland, they couldn't get here any better than Rugar could get off. And with a roomful of hostages, Rugar could probably hold them at bay anyway until he could fly.

If I were Rugar, that would be the best I could think of. Unless he knew stuff I didn't. Which he probably did. Lightning flashed and I could see the big house starkly, and then nothing. I wondered where the Tashtego patrol was. Wherever they were, they weren't doing me any good, and there was no point thinking about them, either. I was at the chapel now, standing close to the building among some large shrubs that thrashed about in the wind. I imagined the chapel inch by inch. Windows, doors, things to hide behind. I bent over and took my gun off my ankle and cleaned it the best I could with my shirttail. Then I held it in against my chest and bent over, shielding it the best I could. It was a revolver, a simple mechanism, not likely to jam, but caution is not a bad thing when it's available.

I edged along the wall to the door that led into the anteroom. With my gun ready, I reached over and turned the handle. The door opened. I stepped in and closed it behind me. The room was dark. I stood stock-still with my gun ready and waited.

Nothing moved. I felt unworldly after so long in the elements. I could hear the storm outside, but by comparison, with the wind shut out, and no rain driving into me, the anteroom seemed preternaturally still. As I stood I could see a hint of light through the peephole in the door opposite, the same door we had peered through earlier when the wedding was to begin.

I walked to it and looked. The room was lit by a pair of big candles on six-foot candlesticks on either side of the entry door at the back of the chapel. Someone had wisely thought to extinguish the others to conserve candles in case they needed more later. Otherwise, everything was much as it had been. The remaining five guys with the MP9s were still along the wall. I could see Susan. She sat perfectly still, looking straight ahead, right where I'd left her. I counted the rows to where she sat. Occasionally an explosion of energy outside caused the candle flames to sway and flicker. Occasionally, as I would check the time, one of the gunmen would look at his watch. The time wasn't going to get better. If Rugar arrived it would get worse.

I took a deep breath and turned and

opened the window behind me. The tempest came howling into the room, and I jumped to the anteroom door and pushed it open and dove onto the floor. The storm howled into the chapel and blew out both candles at once. Some people screamed. One of the guards, nerves shot from waiting, fired an aimless burst at the door. I was well below it, squirming along the floor in the dark behind the back row of pews. Several people stepped on me, probably the gunmen converging on the door. I turned the corner and bellied down the aisle, touching the pews with my left hand as I went. One . . . two . . . three . . . when I got to eight, I rose up and whispered.

"It's me, babe."

Susan's voice said, "Yes."

I put my hand out and touched her thigh, and she took hold of my hand.

"Down," I said, "low, behind me. Door to the right of the altar."

The sudden blast of storm, the darkness, and the burst of gunfire had broken the vow of silence in the chapel, and people were scrambling to get out.

Gun in my right hand, holding Susan's hand with my left, I broke trail, ramming people out of the way as we moved. I couldn't see if they were men or women or gunmen or hostages, but if they were in front of me, I shoved. Then we were at the door, I pushed it open, and we were out into the tempest.

"Now we run," I said.

Susan kicked off her heels, and hanging on to each other, we sprinted away from the chapel into the roaring darkness, toward the barn.

# 11

*There were horses in the barn.* Probably the big Belgians. It was too dark to see them, but as we felt our way along the inside wall, I could hear them moving in their stalls and making that sort of lip-smacking snort that horses make sometimes, for reasons of their own. It was a stone barn, and the thick walls made the storm outside seem more distant. We found a bare space and sat down, our backs against the wall, and breathed for a while. I still had the gun in my right hand, and Susan's hand in my left.

"Do you think they'll find us here?" Susan said.

It was an actual question of interest. Not an expression of fear. Susan could approach hysteria over a bad hair day. But in matters of actual crisis she became calm, and lucid, and penetrating. If they might find us here, we'd best prepare.

"I don't think they'll look," I said. "At the moment, I doubt that anyone in the chapel quite knows what happened. Think about it. The door bursts open. The candles go out. Shots are fired. People scream and run out. Most of their hostages are scattered all over the island."

"What did happen?" Susan said. "I assume it had something to do with you."

"It did," I said. "But you may well be the only one who knows that. For all they know the doors blew open and the rest of it followed."

"So what will they do?"

"It's what Rugar will do," I said. "Once he knows the deal, he'll collect what hostages he has left and assemble them with his shooters by the helicopter. The first moment the storm allows, he'll ditch the hostages, except Adelaide, hop in the chopper with his shooters, and get out of here."

"You're sure?"

"Pretty sure," I said.

"Because?"

"Because that's what I'd do," I said.

"Should we try to stop him?" Susan said.

I loved the "we."

"I have a thirty-eight with five rounds and a two-inch barrel," I said. "Rugar's got five guys with at least thirty rounds each, plus himself, who can shoot the balls off a flea at a hundred yards."

"I don't think fleas have balls," Susan said.

"Their loss," I said.

"Yes," she said.

The barn was warm. The horses generated some heat. And a comforting horsey smell.

"All those circumstances existed when you came to get me," Susan said.

"That's true," I said.

"I get special treatment," she said.

"You do," I said.

"If we get out of this," Susan said, "people may be critical that you didn't save the bride."

"Probably," I said.

"What would you tell them?"

"Never complain," I said. "Never explain."

"No," Susan said. "I want to know."

"I would," I said, "tell them that saving you was all I could manage, and trying to save anyone else would have endangered you."

"And if someone said you sacrificed Adelaide for me, what would you say?"

"I'd say, 'You bet your ass I did.'"

"And you couldn't do both," Susan said.

"No."

"It is one of your greatest strengths," Susan said. "Since I have known you, you do what you can, and do not blame yourself for not doing more."

"There is no red S on my chest," I said. "I cannot leap tall buildings at a single bound."

"Short buildings?" Susan said.

"Short buildings, sure," I said.

"No regrets?"

"None about the buildings," I said.

"But otherwise?"

"Sorrow sometimes. Like when I lost Candy Sloan. But . . ."

"But?" Susan said.

I shrugged, and realized she couldn't see me. It was odd talking like this, two disembodied voices in the oppressive darkness. The lightning flashes seemed to be gone.

"But I did what I could," I said.

"It helps to know that," Susan said, "when you lose."

We were quiet for a time, listening to the horses move pleasantly in their stalls.

"What do you think happened to those security guards?" Susan said.

"Nothing good," I said.

"You think Rugar killed them?"

"Yep."

"Because that's what you would have done."

"If I were Rugar," I said.

"What's interesting is, why you're not."

"Not Rugar?" I said.

"In many ways you're like him," Susan said. "But in crucial ways you're not. It's like Hawk. I've never quite figured it out."

"Hawk's different than Rugar," I said.

"I know," Susan said. "All three of you have rules."

"We do."

"But?" Susan said.

"That's all Rugar's got," I said.

"Hawk has more?"

"Yes," I said.

"And you?"

"I have you," I said.

"I like to think that," Susan said. "But I'm pretty sure you were different than they are before you met me."

"Maybe I was," I said. "But far less happy."

We were quiet again. The horses were quiet. It was hard to be sure, but I thought it possible that the storm was quieting.

"My hair is plastered to my skull," Susan said. "And I'm sure that all my face has washed away."

"Lucky it's dark," I said.

# 12

*At the opposite end* of the barn was a window high up near the peak of the roof. I knew that because it had a little gray light showing though it. Susan was soddenly asleep on the floor beside me. I got up stiffly and walked to the barn door. The horses stirred and muttered. It might have been me walking around, or maybe horses just get hungry early. Outside, except for the uprooted trees and the scattered limbs and the saturated earth, it was as if the world had begun again. The air was clean and still, pungent with the salt smell of the ocean. Nothing moved. To the east the sky was bright with the impending sun. I moved along the edge of the barn with my gun in my hand. The cliff edge was ahead of me. To my left I could see the MP9 that had disappeared in the fight last night. Most of it was washed over with mud, and only the barrel showed. I left it. It would need to be cleaned to be dependable. On the other side of the barn, and at a little distance, I heard the sound of the helicopter starting up. I edged around the corner of the barn and looked toward where I thought it was. It was a lot closer than it had seemed in last night's pitch-black chaos. The blades were turning. And as I watched, the chopper lifted off the ground, hovered for a moment, and then banked away north toward the mainland.

I watched it fly out of sight and then went back inside the barn. The horses were all looking at me.

"I'll make sure somebody feeds you," I said.

Susan had sat up, leaning her back against the wall.

"Who are you talking to?" she said.

"The horses," I said. "They're looking for breakfast."

"And what did you tell them?"

"I said I'd get them fed."

Susan looked at me for a moment, fully awake now.

"My God," she said. "I hope you look worse than I do."

"I always look worse than you do," I said.

"You're a mud ball," she said.

I looked down at myself. All of myself that I could see was caked with mud and grass. I looked at her. Her hair had dried plastered to her skull. The only makeup she had left was her eye makeup, which made dark streaks and splotches on her face. I grinned at her.

"Don't you ever change," I said.

"What were you doing outside?"

"Watching the helicopter take off," I said.

"They're gone?"

"I would say so."

"All of them?"

"I can't imagine a reason to leave anyone here," I said.

**Except the guy at the bottom of the cliff.**

I wondered if he was still there or, more likely, had washed out to sea.

"So presumably, they've got the girl," Susan said.

"Presumably," I said.

"What are we going to do?"

"Reconnoiter," I said.

"I need coffee," Susan said, "and a bath, and a bright mirror, and food."

"That will depend on when the power comes back on," I said.

"Omigod," Susan said. "No coffee? A cold bath?"

"Maybe there's a generator," I said.

We went out of the barn.

"Want to walk with me while I scope out the island," I said. "Make sure."

"Yes," she said. "I don't want to be some-place without you."

"Here we go," I said.

We circled the island. It was a small island. It didn't take long. I carried my gun in my right hand at my side. I was pretty sure all the evildoers had gone. But there was no reason not to be careful. Halfway around the island there was a body. It was one of the Tashtego patrol guys. Susan stopped. I went ahead and knelt down and looked at his storm-soaked body. He'd been shot once, as far as I could see, in the forehead.

I nodded to myself and got up and went back to Susan.

"Dead," I said. "I suspect we'll find the others the same way."

"Rugar?" Susan said.

"Sure," I said. "Keeping busy. While everybody's getting ready for the wedding, he walked around and popped these guys, one at a time."

"They'd have had no reason to be suspicious," Susan said. "So well dressed, so distinguished, just another wedding guest, taking a stroll."

"Yep."

"One at a time," Susan said. "What kind of a man does that?"

"Probably not a people person," I said.

There was another security guy dead behind the chapel. Same bullet hole in his forehead. The chapel itself was empty except for the two bodies near the altar rail. The doors were standing open, the candlesticks tipped over, the flowers scattered, the gauze draping tangled and wet.

We moved on into the main house. The sun was up by now, but even so I could see that lights were on in the house. And I could hear the sound of the generator.

Probably one of those that kicked in automatically when the power went out. The front door was locked, like that would have slowed Rugar down had he wanted to come in. I walked along the front of the house and looked in the floor-to-ceiling windows at the living room. The wedding guests were there, some asleep on the furniture, some asleep on the floor, some staring apprehensively out the window at me. Most of them looked as if they'd spent a lot of time outside in the weather. Sitting quietly in a big wing chair by the fireplace, Heidi saw me and stood. I pointed to the front door, and she nodded and walked toward it and let me in.

"Oh my God," she said. "I thought you were dead. Do you know where Adelaide is?"

"Helicopter took off," I said. "I assume she was aboard."

"Oh, Jesus," Heidi said.

"They took her for a reason," I said. "If they wanted to kill her, they could have done it here."

She nodded.

"Did you have any chance to save her?" she said.

"No," I said.

"I'm sure you did your best," she said.

I nodded.

"Anyone call the cops?" I said.

"Yes. Several people had cell phones. As soon as the candles blew out in the chapel, we all ran out and hid everyplace. The people with cell phones called nine-one-one. But of course the police had no way to get here."

"They'll be along," I said.

"Have the criminals all gone?" Heidi said.

"I just scoped the island," I said, "and found nobody."

"Thank God for small favors," she said.

"Or big ones," I said.

"Are you all right, Dr. Silverman," Heidi said.

"Yes," Susan said.

Heidi studied us for a moment. Her face was pinched, and she looked pallid. But she was not giving in to whatever she felt.

"There's hot water," Heidi said. "I'm going to the kitchen now to see if we can get some sort of breakfast together. See if I can find any of the staff."

Susan and I went to our room, and I got

the first sight of myself in the mirror. I looked like I was in blackface . . . full body.

Susan and I went to the kitchenette, where the floor was made of stone, and took off all our clothes.

"We going to salvage any of your stuff?" I said.

"No," Susan said.

She found a big green plastic bag in the broom closet, and we bundled the clothes up and put them in the bag. I saved my gun and a jackknife that I took from my pants pocket. Susan saved nothing.

There were two bathrooms, at least, in our suite. We each went to one of them and undertook a cleanup. It took me about half an hour. It took Susan much longer.

# 13

*We were clean and sprightly.* We had drunk coffee and eaten sandwiches in the living room, and now we were talking to the cops. The state guys had the duty on the south-coast islands, and there were a lot of them. The first arrivals were a SWAT team in full battle dress who came in by helicopter, much as their opposites had. They went about securing the island. A second chopper brought some EMTs, who tended to people who thought they needed tending to. Later, by boat, almost sedately, came the detectives, led by the state homicide commander, Captain Healy.

When Healy came into the living room and spotted Susan and me, he gestured for us to follow him and we went down the hall to another room, which somebody called the parlor. In my youth the parlor and the living room were one and the same, but my youth was not spent on Tashtego Island.

"Susan," Healy said when we were alone. "If I looked like you, I wouldn't waste my time on the likes of him."

"There are things you don't know," Susan said.

"Or want to," Healy said. Then he turned to me and said, "Okay, tell me what you know."

I told him. He looked at Susan.

"Anything to add?" he said.

She shook her head. He looked back at me.

"Just to be sure I understand," Healy said, "Heidi Bradshaw hired you to be some sort of substitute husband for the wedding."

"What she told me," I said.

"You believe her?"

"No."

Healy looked at Susan.

"You believe her," he said.

"No."

"Either of you have an idea of what she might really have wanted?"

Susan said, "No."

I said, "No idea."

Healy nodded.

"You have had some dealings with the Gray Man before," he said to me.

"Yes."

"Do you think it's a big coincidence that you and he show up on an island off the south coast of Massachusetts?"

"No," I said.

"What do you think it is?" Healy said.

"No idea."

Healy nodded again. He looked at Susan and smiled.

"There you have the essence of my professional life," he said.

"Oddly enough," Susan said, "mine, too."

"You know if Rugar was invited?" Healy said to me.

"I don't know," I said.

"Anything else either of you want to tell me?" Healy said. "Observation? Theory? Anything?"

I shook my head. I could see Susan thinking about it. So could Healy.

"What?" he said to her.

"Just . . . not even an observation . . . an impression, maybe," Susan said.

"Yeah?" Healy said.

"I've seen a lot of traumatized people in my practice," Susan said. "Heidi Bradshaw seems to be holding up awfully well in the face of a horrendous experience culminating in the murder of her son-in-law and the kidnapping of her daughter."

"You think she's somehow involved?" Healy said.

"Perhaps she's simply numb with shock," Susan said. "Perhaps she's Mother Courage. I only can say that her behavior is not consistent with other behavior I've seen in other traumatic circumstances. And I've never seen circumstances as flamboyantly traumatic as these."

Healy looked at me. I shrugged.

"We all know it's hard to assess the performance of people under stress," I said.

Healy was silent. He walked to one of the tall windows and looked out at the storm-littered lawn.

"Well," he said, "we'll see."

He turned back to us from the window.

"You want to go home?" he said.

"Yes," Susan said.

"I'll tell my people at the dock to let you go," Healy said.

Susan said, "Thank you."

Healy looked at me and said, "You going to stay in this?"

"I think I will," I said.

"Thought you might," Healy said. "Just don't muddy the waters."

I grinned at him.

"Can't promise," I said.

"Didn't think you could," Healy said.

# 14

*What with packing and waiting* for a boat and such, we got to Susan's house in the late afternoon. Hawk was there with Pearl. We went in, kissed Pearl, thanked Hawk, fed Pearl, went to bed, and slept for fourteen hours.

In the morning I fed Pearl again and made coffee while Susan prepared a face to meet the patients she would see today. Susan pulled together for work was rather different from the Susan whom I often took to dinner. Work was dark tailored suits, quiet makeup, little jewelry. Dinner was much more glamorous.

And after dinner was sometimes exotic.

At eight-thirty Susan went downstairs for her first patient. Pearl and I went out and ran along the river. We were back to Susan's by nine-thirty. We were in my office checking the mail by ten. Actually, I was checking the mail. Pearl was on her couch against the far wall, resting her eyes.

The mail was unenlightening, though a couple of clients paid their bills, which was pleasing. There were no phone messages, no e-mail except spam. I wondered if anyone ever bought anything as a result of being spammed. I hoped not.

I got out a lined yellow pad and a Bic pen and sat, and looked out the window at the place where Berkeley Street crosses Boylston. Or does Boylston cross Berkeley? Either way, the storm that had hit Tashtego full-on had then followed the coastline out along the cape and on out to sea. Boston had gotten only rain. The rain had been heavy and had washed everything so that the old redbrick city seemed to glow in the Indian-summer sunshine.

I wrote *Heidi Bradshaw* on my pad.

Then I sat some more and looked out the window.

Then I wrote *Peter Van Meer* on my pad. And in a creative frenzy wrote down *Maurice Lessard* and *Adelaide Van Meer Lessard*. Then I looked out the window some more.

It was odd for the Gray Man to be involved in a simple kidnapping for ransom, even one as ornate as this one. And if he was going to kidnap her, why would he not wait until she was on her way home from Wal-Mart, or Tiffany, or wherever Adelaide shopped, and grab her. Why a kidnapping that required a squad of submachine gunners and a helicopter, in front of a host of celebrated people, on an island that had limited exit choices?

"Why is that?" I said to Pearl.

Pearl, who was lying on her back with her feet in the air and her head lolling off the couch, opened her eyes for a moment and looked at me upside down, and closed her eyes again.

"Lassie woulda known," I said.

I got up and made some coffee and stood in my bay window and looked down while it brewed. Then I poured myself a cup with cream and sugar and sat back down and put my feet up.

I drank some coffee.

Did Rugar want it to be noticeable? Or did someone who hired Rugar want that? Did they want to sell the kidnapping? Why would they want to? Why would they think they needed to? And why Rugar? Rugar was the big leagues. Whoever wanted her kidnapped could have hired any third-rate fringe guy to grab her. How did they even know about Rugar? You didn't find him hanging on a corner in South Philly.

I drank some more coffee.

Maybe I was looking the wrong way. Maybe the kidnapping was a decoy. On my yellow pad I wrote *DEATHS: Minister, Maurice Lessard, four Tashtego patrol guys, the shooter I threw off the cliff.* Others? The guy off the cliff could not be planned for. I crossed him out. The security guys almost certainly just drew the wrong duty at the wrong time. Hard to imagine that this whole elaborate charade was a cover to kill one or more of them. I knew nothing about the minister. If there were others, Healy would let me know. Healy was meticulous. He would run down everybody. And he would share it with me. We went back a long way, and while we weren't exactly friends, we weren't exactly not friends. More than that, Healy was not a protocol guy. If anyone could help him, he'd take the help.

I stood again and looked down at Berkeley Street. It was lunchtime, and lots of people, many of them well-dressed young women, were on the street, going to lunch. I examined them closely, but none looked suspicious.

I sat down again. I poured some more coffee. I drank some and stared out the window some more. Then I picked up my pen and crossed out everybody on my yellow pad but Heidi and Adelaide, Peter Van Meer, and Maurice Lessard.

"Solid gumshoe technique," I said to Pearl. "Narrow the investigation."

Pearl didn't even open an eye. She usually paid very little attention to discussions that did not involve food or a walk. She paid very little attention to this one.

# 15

Healy came into my office without knocking, carrying a briefcase, and sat down in one of the client chairs that I had arranged hopefully in front of my desk. He opened the briefcase, took out a blue manila folder, and tossed it onto my desk.

"Background," Healy said. "The results of our extensive research."

"Folder looks kind of thin," I said.

"I knew you'd be grateful," Healy said.

I slid the folder toward myself and left it closed on the desktop.

"Can't wait to read it," I said. "Is there a ransom request yet?"

"Not to my knowledge."

"You think they'd tell you?" I said.

"I think so."

"Even if they were warned not to?" I said.

"Most people are so shook by the whole thing they want to turn it over to us regardless."

I nodded.

"Unless they can hire some guy like you," Healy said.

"There is no guy like me," I said. "Except me."

"And you don't know anything about a ransom."

"No," I said.

"And you'd tell me if you did," Healy said.

"Maybe," I said.

"Ah," Healy said. "The spirit of cooperation."

"What else you got?" I said.

"The final body count," Healy said, "not counting the guy you say went off the cliff, we haven't found him yet, is six."

I counted on my fingers.

"The minister," I said, "the groom, four security guys."

"Shot?"

"Yep," Healy said. "Single shot to the head, all of them."

"Same gun?" I said.

"Probably," Healy said. "We can't find a couple of the slugs, and some of the ones we did find are so mangled from ricocheting around inside the vic that the lab can't do anything with them. The ones we can use all came from the same nine-millimeter weapon."

"Rugar had a Glock," I said.

Healy nodded.

"Six people," Healy said.

"In an afternoon," I said.

Healy nodded.

"You find out where the chopper landed?" I said.

"No."

"Hard to land one where nobody notices," I said.

"Easy if you do it where choppers come and go all day," Healy said.

"Good point," I said.

"Minister was head of some big-time Episcopal church in NYC," Healy said. "The groom is from a very wealthy family in Philadelphia. Pharmaceuticals. Father is very active in Republican politics. He was an ambassador somewhere, and then he was secretary of something for a while."

"Which is his reward for being active," I said.

"I wonder what the punishment would be," Healy said.

"I know," I said. "I wouldn't want to do it, either. What did the kid do?"

"Vice president of one of the companies," Healy said.

"How old was he?"

"Twenty-three," Healy said. "Worked his way up."

"If you're going to practice nepotism," I said, "you may as well keep it in the family. Where'd he go to school?"

"Penn," Healy said.

"How'd he meet Adelaide?"

"Mutual friend," Healy said. "It's in the folder."

"How about the Tashtego patrol guys?" I said.

"Usual. Two of them were cops in Westport, one had been in the Marines, one was an MP. All of them had a little college. Enough so they could talk to rich people without falling down."

"Anything not usual?" I said.

"Nothing. No connection we could find to anyone. No criminal record, any of them. The security service was bonded."

"Any of them get off a shot?" I said.

"No."

"Clear the holster?"

"No."

We were quiet for a while.

"He's a piece of work," Healy said finally.

"Rugar?

Healy nodded.

"Six people," he said. "In a couple of hours."

We were quiet again.

Then I said, "Whaddya think?"

Healy shook his head.

"It's the worst way to kidnap somebody I've ever seen," Healy said.

"And no ransom demand," I said. "And didn't they have any idea there'd be a damn typhoon?"

"I checked," Healy said. "Weather people said it would miss us."

"Of course they did," I said.

"This smells bad," Healy said. "The only thing that keeps it from smelling worse is that it's so loony that maybe we're missing something."

"Rugar is no amateur," I said.

"That bothers me, too," Healy said. "And you bother me. What the fuck were you there for?"

"Arm candy?" I said.

"Besides that," Healy said.

"I don't know," I said. "You ask her?"

"I did. She told me the same crap about having a man at her side that she told you."

"I bet she knows a lot of men," I said.

"It's like a radio signal, isn't it?" Healy said.

"Loud and clear," I said.

"So why hire one?" Healy said.

"She must have wanted a guy with my skill set," I said.

"Must be the case," Healy said. "But she's got a security force on the island. Why hire you?"

"Because I am more powerful than a speeding locomotive?"

"But not as smart," Healy said. "Be nice to know what she thought your skill set was."

"I could ask her," I said.

"And you could ask whoever recommended you to her," Healy said.

"If we knew," I said.

"You're a detective," Healy said. "Maybe you can find out."

"Okay," I said. "I'll ask around."

# 16

*Neither Quirk nor Belson* had had any contact with Heidi Bradshaw. In fact, Belson claimed not to know who she was.

"For crissake, Frank," I said. "That's like not knowing who Jackie Onassis was."

"Who?" Belson said.

I think he was kidding.

I sat for a while with my feet up on my desk. Someone like Heidi would probably ask her lawyer. Her lawyers probably weren't the kind who would know about the likes of me. So they'd call someone. Probably a criminal lawyer. The best one

in this part of the country was Rita Fiore.
I called her.

"You know who Heidi Bradshaw is?" I
said.

"Of course."

"She or anyone representing her get
in touch with you and ask for a super-
hero?"

"As an attorney at law," Rita said, "I am
bound by the ethics of my profession to
reveal nothing to you without at least ex-
tracting lunch."

"I like a person with standards," I said.
"Grill 23 in an hour?"

"Upstairs," she said. "It's more intimate."

"Intimate," I said.

*I got there first,* climbed the curving staircase, and was at a table for four in a quiet
corner, drinking iced tea, when Rita showed
up. She might not have quite equaled
Susan for gorgeous, but she was certainly
as noticeable. A lot of thick auburn hair,
some sort of close-fitting green outfit with
a skirt that stopped above the knees, and
boots that stopped below them.

Close-fitting is not always good news
with lawyers, but Rita was quite precisely

designed for it. She had large sunglasses pushed up onto her head, and was carrying a purse that would work as a hammock for Pygmies. She put the purse on an empty chair and sat down next to me. She leaned over and kissed me carefully, not messing up her lip gloss.

"My calendar is clear for the afternoon," she said. "Shall we order champagne?"

"Between husbands?" I said.

"Even if I weren't," she said.

"Tea's good for you," I said.

"That's what they said about spinach," Rita said.

When the waiter arrived she ordered a champagne cocktail.

"So did you recommend my services to anyone?" I said.

"When I was a prosecutor," she said, "in Norfolk County, I knew a guy in the same office named Jimmy Gabriel. He's now the managing partner in the firm of Gabriel and Whitcomb in New Bedford."

The waiter brought Rita her cocktail. She sampled it, looked pleased, and put it down.

"He called me and said that Heidi Bradshaw was looking for a smart, tough, presentable guy to be with her for a three-day wedding weekend. Tough and presentable, you were an easy choice," Rita said. "I choked a little on smart but couldn't think of anybody else."

"He say why she wanted me?"

"No. I warned him that I had been trying for about twenty years to get you to spend a three-day weekend with me, but that you were the functional equivalent of married. He said that Heidi's interests weren't sexual."

"Damn," I said.

"Yeah," Rita said, "I know. It's disappointing to hear, isn't it?"

"What kind of a firm is Gabriel and Whitcomb?" I said.

"One that specializes in clients who can afford them," Rita said.

"In New Bedford?" I said.

"Not a wealthy city, but there's money along the south coast."

"I could see that," I said. "And you didn't want to give me a heads-up?"

Rita shook her head. She had picked up her glass again and was looking at me over it.

"I wanted you to say yea or nay on its own merits. I know you. You believe in favors. If you thought I wanted you to do it, or needed you to do it, you'd do it."

I nodded. Rita sipped her champagne cocktail. Then she put it down and leaned her forearms on the table and looked at me for a long moment.

"You were there, I assume, when the ball went up," she said.

"Yep."

"What did you do?" Rita said.

"Mostly I wandered around in the hurricane like Lear on the heath," I said.

"Change places and handy dandy," Rita said.

"Which is the justice," I said, "which is the thief?"

"Think we got the quotes right?"

"Close enough," I said.

"Was Susan there?"

"Yes," I said.

"I'll bet your heath wandering was in her interest," Rita said.

"You think?" I said.

"You are as predictable as sunrise."

"Or sunset," I said.

"I'm a glass-half-full girl," Rita said. "Even though you have rejected me for twenty years."

"It hasn't been easy," I said.

"That's comforting," Rita said.

She opened her menu.

"They have the best meatloaf in the known universe," I said.

"For lunch?" Rita said.

"Sometimes."

"A nice salad will do for me," she said. "Criminal defense lawyers shouldn't have a fat ass."

"You seem in little danger," I said.

"How would you know?" she said.

"I pay close attention to such matters," I said.

"Not close enough," she said.

"Well, I have a lot of eyewitness testimony to support my position," I said.

Rita giggled, which was always fun to see.

"Oh, fuck you," she said.

"Or not," I said.

She giggled again.

"How long have we been dancing this dance?" Rita said.

"More than twenty years," I said.

"And I've never gotten you into bed," she said.

"Not many men can claim that," I said.

She put her hand out and I put mine on top of it.

"I hope the music never stops," she said.

I patted her hand for a moment.

"They don't seem to have meatloaf on the lunch menu today," I said.

"Life is not without disappointment," Rita said.

"So far," I said.

We were quiet.

Then Rita said, "You want me to call Jimmy? Tell him you'll be stopping by?"

"If you would," I said.

# 17

*Gabriel and Whitcomb* had offices in a recycled warehouse near the waterfront. Old brick, exposed beams, a lot of hanging greenery, some stained glass. It could have been a cocktail lounge in San Diego. From his corner office, Jimmy could look out at the bridge to Fairhaven, where the waters of the Acushnet River began to mingle with the harbor. On a small sideboard near the windows were pictures of a handsome blonde woman in golf clothes, and two soon-to-be-handsome blonde girls in riding clothes.

Jimmy himself was slim and sharp-faced with longish black hair combed straight back. He wore a blue blazer and a white shirt, no tie, gray slacks, and black loafers, no socks. There was a Rolex on his left wrist. Casual elegance. His dark eyes studied me with piercing sincerity.

"Any friend of Rita's," he said.

"Rita has a lot of friends," I said.

"You got that right," Jimmy said.

His smile was wide and warm, and just as sincere as his eyes.

"You represent Heidi Bradshaw," I said.

"The firm does," Jimmy said.

"In all legal matters?"

"Oh, God, no," Jimmy said. "At her level, she needs all sorts of expertise. We are sort of legal triage for her; we field her problems, solve them when it's our area, find the right people to solve them if it's another area."

"Which is how you got to me," I said.

"We respect Rita's recommendation, and may I say, hers for you was absolutely glowing."

"And richly deserved," I said. "Why did Heidi want someone in the first place?"

Jimmy did several noncommittal things with his head, shoulders, and hands.

"Heidi is Heidi," he said.

"I noticed that," I said. "What did she say she wanted someone for?"

"Goddamn," Jimmy said. "I'm sorry. But I can't . . . you know, privilege and all that."

"How did she phrase her request to you?" I said.

"Geez," Jimmy said, "you were there, weren't you, for all the trouble."

"I was," I said.

"God, I'm sorry. What a tragedy."

"How did she ask for the someone that turned out to be me?" I said.

"God, Spenser, I'm sorry. I really am," Jimmy said. "Rita told me about you when she called to say you'd be coming by."

"That I was articulate and charming?"

"She said that you wouldn't let it alone. That since you were there you'd take it personal and all that. I know you are just trying to find Adelaide."

"I am," I said.

"But I can't talk about clients, you know? I start doing that, how many do I have left after a while?"

I nodded.

"So you probably won't fill me in on her marriages, her relationships with her ex-husbands, her relationship with her daughter, her son-in-law, his family, her financial circumstances, her sex life, her social life. Friends? Booze? Drugs? Gamble? Debt?"

"Oh my God, no," Jimmy said. "Jesus . . . no comment. No fucking comment."

I nodded.

"Rita said you asked for someone smart, tough, and presentable," I said.

Jimmy recovered from his horror sufficiently to smile self-effacingly.

"The firm's language," he said.

"But I assume she didn't ask for stupid, fearful, and repellent," I said.

"We tried to rephrase her accurately," Jimmy said. "Obviously, you're the kind of guy she had in mind."

"And wasn't I useful," I said.

"I'm sure you did what you could," Jimmy said. "One man . . ."

I nodded.

"And you had your girlfriend to look out for," Jimmy said.

I nodded. Apparently, Jimmy knew more

than he pretended to about the stormy night on Tashtego.

"You arrange the Tashtego security patrol?" I said.

"We located the proper company for her, and made the deal."

"What's the company?"

Jimmy thought about it for a moment, and decided it was not in violation of his sacred honor to tell me.

"Absolute Security," he said. "In Providence."

"Who do I talk to?"

"Artie Fonseca," Jimmy said. "He's the CEO."

"Who might want something like this to happen?" I said.

"The killing, the kidnapping? I assume some psychopath thought he could make some money."

I shook my head.

"I know the guy who ran the operation," I said. "He probably wouldn't do a kidnapping for money. There are a lot of easier ways. And if he did do a kidnapping for money, he wouldn't do it this way. Helicopters, for crissake?"

"You think somebody hired him?"

"I do."

"Who on earth . . . ?"

"My question exactly," I said.

## 18

**"I lost four guys," Fonseca said.**

"Sorry about that," I said.

"I don't like it," Fonseca said. "Losing people."

"It's tough," I said.

"I don't like it," he said.

He was a spare, middle-sized man with a shaved head and a big mustache. He looked in shape.

"Tell me about the operation," I said.

"The patrol?"

"The patrol," I said. "The company. Anything that might be useful."

"We do business around the country. Rich, low-profile people mostly, estate security, bodyguards . . . you know."

"Heidi Bradshaw is hardly low-profile."

"Her money's as good as if she were," Fonseca said.

"Do any investigation?"

"Nope, strictly protection," Fonseca said.

"Ever run into anything like this before?" I said.

"No."

"How'd it work?" I said.

"Tashtego? Three four-man patrols plus a supervisor. When the guys got killed it was the second shift. Two Jeeps. Two guys in a Jeep. Radio. Sidearms. One shotgun per Jeep. Locked in a mount."

"Supervisor?" I said.

"No. He only works during the day. Senior guy was in charge."

"He was?"

"Chet. Chester DeMarco, one of the guys killed."

"How many people do you employ?" I said.

"You mean overall?"

"Yeah," I said. "Whole company."

"Two hundred eighty-seven," he said. "Plus the home office staff of thirteen, myself included."

"Who knew about the Tashtego operation?" I said.

"Home office, guys on Tashtego, I don't know, some others, I'm sure. It wasn't secret or anything."

"You have files on all your employees?"

"Your guys got them already," he said.

"My guys?"

"Couple Massachusetts detectives came in, borrowed all the records."

"Okay," I said. "They'll do all the fact-crunching. Leaves me to do the genius stuff."

Fonseca looked at me. He had shiny blue eyes that looked almost metallic.

"You do much of that?" he said.

"Genius stuff?" I said. "Hardly any."

He nodded.

"They were okay guys," Fonseca said. "You know? Guys like you play ball with, drink beer, talk about broads. Ordinary. They all had some experience. Cops, military. None of them had a record. All of them were trained . . . not one of them cleared his piece."

"They were up against something un-usual," I said.

"Guy that pulled this off, what's his name, Rugar?"

"That's the one he was using when he pulled it off," I said.

"You need anything from me to help catch him," Fonseca said, "you got it."

I nodded.

"If you need one," Fonseca said, "I can put together a small army. Pretty good men. Some women, too. None of them happy about this."

"I'll keep it in mind," I said.

"Cops told me no ransom demand yet."

"That's what they tell me, too," I said.

"So what kind of kidnapping is this?" Fonseca said. "Why didn't they just wait until after the honeymoon and grab her off the street on her way to the supermarket."

"I doubt that she goes to the supermarket," I said.

"Or the polo field? Wherever people like her fucking go," Fonseca said.

"I don't know," I said. "Anyone say anything to you about me being there?"

"At the wedding?"

"Yeah."

"Nope," he said.

"She didn't ask you for a referral?"

"Nope."

"You'd be the logical choice," I said.

"If it was a security question," Fonseca said. "Maybe it wasn't."

"Or maybe she thought you wouldn't like her hiring somebody else."

"Maybe," Fonseca said.

"You know Jimmy Gabriel?"

Fonseca shrugged.

"Professionally," Fonseca said. "He put us together with Ms. Bradshaw."

"You like him?"

"He's a freakin' lawyer," Fonseca said.

"That makes it hard," I said.

"Don't *dis*like him," Fonseca said.

"Any thoughts on why she might have wanted me there?"

"Don't know why she wanted you there," Fonseca said.

"Me, either," I said.

"Didn't make much difference," Fonseca said.

Through the big window in the wall behind Fonseca's ornately carved cherry-wood desk, I could see the Providence

River where it passed through the down-town.

"No," I said. "None at all."

Fonseca took a business card from a small holder on his desk and slid it across to me.

"Offer holds," Fonseca said. "Any help I can give you, finding that fucking Rugar, I'll do it."

I picked up the card and put it in my shirt pocket.

"You got a card?" Fonseca said.

I gave him one of mine.

"You ever do security work?" Fonseca said.

"Not really. Bodyguard now and then."

"Well, you got the build for it," Fonseca said. "Used to box, too, didn't you."

"Face give it away?" I said.

"Uh-huh. Around the eyes a little, and the nose."

"You ever box?" I said to Fonseca.

"Not really," he said. "We all do a little martial-arts training in the company, 'cept the secretaries, but I never did any boxing. I might need a guy like you sometime. I'll give you a call."

"Sure."

"What you gonna do now?" Fonseca said.

"I've asked everybody else why Ms. Bradshaw hired me. I guess I may as well go ask her."

"Good thinking," Fonseca said.

# 19

*Susan was busy trying to help* the deranged, so she didn't come with me to Tashtego again. Too bad. I was interested in seeing how her relationship with Heidi would develop. Susan did not like women who flirted with me in front of her, or, I assume, at other times, but at other times the issue didn't come up. She was also far too classy to let it show, and I was always fascinated at the thoughtful solutions to that problem that she came up with. However, her location, in the heart of Cambridge, gave her a huge market for her skills, and in the fall, when Harvard was cranked up to its maximum silliness, Susan had very little free time.

The Tashtego patrol had obviously been augmented since the wedding. There was a security search on the dock in New Bedford before we went on the launch.

"Can't go aboard with a weapon," the security guy said. "We'll hold it here for you."

I didn't argue. Gun hadn't done a hell of a lot for me last time.

There were guards with shotguns on the launch. On the island, one man in each Jeep carried his shotgun on his lap. No antebellum carriage ride for me this time. I got in the front seat of one of the Jeeps. The guy with the shotgun sat behind me in the backseat.

"There's cocktails in the atrium," Maggie Lane said when I presented myself at the door. "Heidi has asked that you join us."

Heidi was, apparently, not in seclusion. Maggie led me briskly down the hall. I hated briskly. When I wasn't rushed, I liked to saunter. She paused at the atrium door to wait for me. She didn't say anything, and her face didn't show anything. But her shoulders looked impatient. I could hear

the sound of a stringed instrument and the
low sound of elegant conversation.

"Before I plunge into the social whirl," I
said, "how did you happen to get this job
with Heidi?"

"We both went to Lydia Hall College,"
Maggie said. "Though we weren't there at
the same time. But when Heidi was looking for an assistant she called the place-
ment office, and they sent me out, and
we . . ." Maggie spread her hands to imply
that the rest was history.

"You know when she graduated?" I said.

"Oh, before my time. Nineteen eighty,
maybe."

"What was her maiden name?" I said.

Maggie looked slightly startled.

"Maiden name? Before she got mar-
ried?" Maggie said. "Hell, I don't know.
When she hired me her name was Heidi
Van Meer."

"First husband?" I said.

"Second, I believe."

"And Bradshaw?"

"Current husband," Maggie said. "Estranged."

Maggie opened the door and stepped
aside, and I went in past her. The room

was amazing. It was all glass, including the domed roof, and in all directions it offered a view of the Atlantic Ocean stretching empty into the distance, hinting of eternity. The men wore blazers in various tones of blue and brown, green and gray, striped and solid. Most of them wore white or pale tan slacks. The women were in little cocktail dresses, some black, some flowered, all showing a lot of suntanned arms, backs, shoulders, and chests. A woman in a long, roomy white dress was in an alcove against the wall of the main house, playing a large harp and using a lot of wrist flourish to do it. She had a flower in her hair.

There was a bar near the harpist, and a bartender in a white jacket and a black bow tie. There were two cocktail waitresses dressed in the short-skirted black dress, white apron getup that had been the staple of dirty French-maid postcards in my early youth. At the far window, with her hair piled high, and the sun shimmering on her jewelry, wearing a very minimal white cocktail dress and very high heels, Heidi Bradshaw was talking to a man with shoulder-length blond hair who looked like he might be the

lead dancer for the Chippendales. He was
stuffed into a wheat-colored unstructured
linen jacket over a maroon polo shirt with
the collar turned up. They were sipping
something that from where I stood looked
like mojitos.

Heidi saw me and waved and gestured
me over. I went.

"Here you are," she said, and gave me
a small air kiss near my cheek. "This is
Clark."

I said, "Hello, Clark."

He nodded. Probably too muscular to
speak.

"Clark's looking out for me," Heidi said.

"That's nice," I said.

One of the French maids came by with
a tray.

"Mojito, sir?" she said.

"No, thank you," I said.

"Oh, don't be a poop," Heidi said. "Have
a drink."

"I don't care much for mojitos," I said.

Clark looked like he wanted to smack me
for not liking mojitos. But he contained it.

"Bring Mr. Spenser something he likes,"
Heidi said to the waitress.

The waitress looked at me.

"Beer would be swell," I said.

"Yes, sir," she said, and she walked away toward the bar. I watched her. She did a nice walk-away.

"Could we take a few minutes to talk?" I said.

"About what?" she said.

"About your daughter, that sort of thing," I said.

"That is of no further concern to you," she said. "I asked my accountant to pay you. Has he not done so?"

"He has," I said. "Have you heard anything from your daughter's kidnappers?"

"I prefer not to talk about it," Heidi said.

"Why did you agree to see me?" I said.

"I was trying to be agreeable. I didn't want you to think that I was angry with you for failing to prevent the awful thing that happened. I just thought you'd stop by, have a drink, and we'd part on good terms."

My beer arrived. Heineken. I took the bottle, left the glass on the tray. In a minute, I knew, I was going to hear from Clark. I was annoyed. I knew nothing, and the more I nosed around, the less I knew. I had no idea what Heidi was doing. I was

being lied to. I didn't like that. I didn't like
the growing suspicion that I had been used
in some capacity I couldn't figure out. And
I didn't like Clark. I didn't like his hair, or his
linen jacket, or his stand-up collar, or his
square jaw. I didn't like his tan, or his mus-
cles, or the honey-colored woven-leather
loafers he had on. I didn't like his proprietary glare. Or his erroneous assumption
that he could knock me down and kick me
if he needed to.

"Do you have any idea where your
daughter is?" I said.

"I've answered that already," she said.

"What did you hire me for?" I said.

"I regret that I did," she said.

"Me, too," I said. "But the question
stands."

She looked at the Chippendale.

"Clark?" she said.

He nodded.

"Ms. Bradshaw has told you she don't
wish to speak of it," he said. "You'll have to
leave."

I had a brief internal struggle, which I
lost. I was too frustrated.

"What's option B?" I said.

"I remove you," Clark said.

"I'll take that one," I said.

"What?"

"I'll take option B," I said. "Remove me."

Clark looked at Heidi. Heidi had an odd look on her face.

"Remove Mr. Spenser, Clark."

He was so spectacularly big and muscular that it probably didn't occur to him that he couldn't. Most times he probably just frightened people into submission. He put his left hand flat against my chest and pushed.

"Okay," he said. "Move it."

I brought both hands up and knocked his hand away, which left both my hands up, and in convenient position for step two. Clark initiated step two by throwing a big roundhouse right hand at me. I deflected it with my left and stepped back.

"Clark," I said. "That's not the way."

He lunged at me and I put a stiff jab on his nose.

"Get your feet under you," I said. "Left one forward."

I gave him another jab and ducked under his left and moved to my right.

"See, if you don't have your legs under

you, you don't turn well. Which lets me get around you and bang up your body."

I hooked him left, then right, to the ribs. I heard him gasp. He wouldn't last long, even if I didn't hit him. There's shape, and there's fighting shape. Clark was maybe in posing shape. He was already starting to suck air. He was slower throwing the big right again. I brushed it away with my left.

"And don't loop your punches," I said. "Lead with your hip. Keep your elbows in. Guy your size, you should be working in close anyway, use your muscle."

I doubled up on a jab to the nose and then stepped in and hit him a big right-hand uppercut, and Clark fell over.

"See how I started my hip first?" I said. "And let the punch follow it?"

Clark wasn't out. But he was through. He sat on the floor. I knew his head was swimming. He was breathing as hard as he could.

"The companions you hire," I said to Heidi, "don't seem to be working out."

Her face was a little flushed. Her eyes were shiny. She ran the tip of her tongue along her lower lip. I turned and walked out of the atrium. Behind me the harpist was still playing. As I walked down the hall toward the front door, two security guards came in, walking fast.

"What happened," one of them said to me.

"Clark just got knocked on his ass," I said.

"Good," he said, and kept on past me into the atrium.

# 20

*"Well,"* Susan said. "That worked out swell."

It was Sunday morning. We were in her kitchen. She was sipping her coffee, watching me make clam hash for breakfast.

"Nothing ventured, nothing gained," I said.

"And what was gained from this venture?" she said.

"The considerable satisfaction of giving Clark a big smack," I said.

"That's why your right hand seems swollen."

"I deserve it," I said. "The uppercut was

showing off. Another minute or so and he'd have run out of oxygen."

"It didn't seem to bother you earlier this morning," Susan said. "Does it hurt?"

"Only if I punch somebody."

"Which you do much less of these days," Susan said.

"I'm maturing," I said.

"But not aging," Susan said.

I smiled at her.

"You're thinking about earlier this morning, aren't you."

"Hard not to," Susan said.

I was chopping onions.

"Is there a pun in there?"

"Not unless you are a lecherous pig," Susan said.

"Oink," I said.

"And bless you for it," Susan said. "You might have learned some things. You said Heidi Bradshaw acted strangely."

"The fight excited her," I said.

"Fights can be exciting?"

"There was something wrong with her excitement," I said. "Her eyes. There was something going on in her eyes."

"Like what?" Susan said.

I mixed the chopped onions with the clams.

"Like I was peeking in a window and seeing something terrible," I said.

"I guess you had to be there," Susan said.

I nodded. I cubed some boiled red potatoes, skins and all, and stirred them in with the chopped clams and onions.

"There's something else, now that I'm thinking about it," I said.

"Yes," she said. "I think there is."

"You know what it is?" I said.

"Yes," Susan said. "If you're reporting accurately."

"I always report accurately," I said.

She nodded.

"I know," she said. "Heidi's behavior is inconsistent with all the things that have happened."

"Wow," I said.

Susan smiled.

"Harvard," she said, "Ph.D."

"Yet still sexually active," I said.

"You should know," Susan said.

"I should," I said. "Right after the kidnapping you remarked that her reactions seemed odd, but we both know that shock can cause all sorts of behavior."

"Yes," Susan said. "But the shock should have worn off by now. Her current behavior should be far more genuine."

"Cocktails in the atrium," I said. "A new companion."

"Or bodyguard," Susan said. "However ineffective."

"I wasn't too effective, either," I said.

"Hard to decide that," Susan said, "without knowing exactly what you were supposed to effect."

I nodded.

"And it seemed like an inside job," I said.

"You've always wanted to say that, haven't you?"

"Detectives are supposed to say stuff like that," I said. "And it had to be inside. Rugar wouldn't have taken a job without knowing the layout. Who was where. What the security was. What time things were happening."

"You think Heidi was involved in kidnapping her own daughter?"

"If that's what it was," I said.

"What it was?"

"I'm just noodling," I said. "But what if

the kidnapping was a head fake. What if the real business was something else?"

"What?"

"The murder of the clergyman . . . or the son-in-law . . . or a scheme to extract ransom from somebody, like Adelaide's father."

"And you think Heidi could be involved?"

"I don't know," I said. "That's why I'm noodling. It doesn't have to be Heidi. It could be anybody who knew what was going on. Maggie Lane, the famous conductor . . . Adelaide."

"Wow, you are noodling," Susan said.

"Better a theory," I said, "than nothing."

"Theory is no substitute for information," Susan said.

"They certainly didn't teach you that at Harvard," I said.

Susan smiled.

"No," she said. "Some things I know, I learned from you."

# 21

*Lydia Hall College* was north of New York City, near Greenwich, Connecticut. About a three-hour drive from Boston, unless you stopped at Rein's Deli for a tongue sandwich on light rye. So it was almost four hours after I left home that I was in the alumni office talking to a very presentable woman named Ms. Gold.

"At various times," I said, "her name has been Heidi Washburn, Heidi Van Meer, and currently, Heidi Bradshaw."

"Marriages?" Ms Gold said.

"Yes," I said. "All to men of substance, I believe."

Ms. Gold smiled.

"The best kind," she said. "And what is your interest?"

"You know who Heidi Bradshaw is?" I said.

"I've heard of her," Ms. Gold said.

"Then you know of the recent kidnapping?"

"Of her daughter," Ms. Gold said. "Yes."

"I'm involved in that investigation," I said.

"Are you a police officer?" Ms. Gold said.

"Private detective," I said.

"Do you have any identification?" Ms. Gold said.

I showed her some. She looked at it and handed it back.

"We do not normally give out information about our alumni," she said.

"I really only want to know that she is an alumna, and what her maiden name is."

Ms. Gold looked like she approved of my use of *alumna*.

"Well, I think we can tell you that," she said. "We'll take up the maiden-name business later."

"She may have graduated in 1980," I said.

She turned to the desktop computer and worked it for a while.

"We have no Heidi Van Meer. We have a Heidi Washburn, but she graduated in 1926. And we have a Heidi Bradshaw who graduated in 2001."

"How about under her husbands' names," I said, and gave her the names that were in Healy's background folder. "Mrs. Peter Van Meer. Mrs. J. Taylor Washburn. Mrs. Harden Bradshaw?"

She did the computer thing again.

"No," she said.

Her voice lingered on the *no.*

"But?" I said.

"Let me think a moment," Ms. Gold said.

I waited. She was ash-blonde and slim. She wore a pair of glasses with big blue frames. She was nicely dressed in a tasteful well-tailored cashmere-and-tweed kind of way. There was a wedding ring on the appropriate finger. After a time she exhaled softly.

"Do you suspect Heidi Bradshaw of involvement?" she said.

"I don't know," I said. "I'm collecting information."

"Who are you working for?"

"This is pro bono," I said.

"Really? I was under the impression that everyone involved is wealthy."

"I was there when the kidnapping went down, and couldn't prevent it," I said.

"And it rankles you?" she said.

"It does."

"So you are investigating basically in service to your own self-regard?" she said.

"You could say so."

"Your self-regard seems very high," she said.

"And I want to keep it that way," I said.

She nodded and smiled and sat another moment.

"We have a senior faculty member named J. Taylor Washburn," she said.

"Was he married to someone named Heidi?" I said.

"I don't know. It just seemed a sufficient coincidence that I should tell you."

"Would it be in your best interest," I said, "if I didn't tell anyone how I learned of Professor Washburn?"

"His existence is hardly a secret," Ms. Gold said. "He's listed in our catalog."

"Can you tell if she ever attended this college?" I said.

"If she did, it is unlikely that we wouldn't have her," Ms. Gold said.

"Even if she didn't graduate?"

"This office is about acquiring money for the college," Ms. Gold said. "Once you are no longer a student, you become alumni, which is to say a source of revenue."

"So you are quite assiduous," I said.

Ms. Gold smiled.

"Like wolverines," she said.

# 22

*Professor J. Taylor Washburn* had a B.A. from Penn and a Ph.D. from Columbia. He was an art historian. He taught a graduate seminar in low-country realism, and was the chairman of the Fine Arts Department.

I learned all of this in the first five minutes of our conversation. I also learned that he had once been married to a young woman named Hilda Gretsky.

"Was she a student here?" I said.

"No," Washburn said. "I met her at a gallery."

"In the city?"

"Yes," Washburn said, "downtown. One of my teaching assistants was having a show. Sadly, it was not very good."

Washburn appeared to be about sixty, with wavy snow-white hair worn longish. His complexion was red, and his thick white mustache was carefully trimmed.

"When were you married?"

"Nineteen eighty," Washburn said.

"How long did it last?"

Washburn looked out the window at the open quadrangle in the center of the campus with the redbrick Georgian library at one end and the redbrick Georgian student union at the other.

"Two years," he said.

"What occasioned the breakup," I said.

He kept looking out the window.

"She asked me for a divorce," he said. "She told me she'd been having an affair with a man named Van Meer."

"Must have been hard to hear," I said.

"Yes."

I took a picture of Heidi from my pocket and put it on his desk.

"Is this Hilda Gretsky?" I said.

He looked at the photograph.

"Yes," he said.

"Are you aware of who she's become?" I said.

"Yes."

"Do you know when she began to call herself Heidi?" I said.

"When I knew her she called herself Heidi. The name on her birth certificate and her marriage license was Hilda, but she always hated the name, and always introduced herself as Heidi."

"How old is she?" I said.

"She was born in 1959," Washburn said.

"She from New York?" I said.

He shook his head.

"Dayton, Ohio," he said.

"Why did she come to New York?" I said.

He stopped looking out the window and turned to me and smiled without much pleasure.

"To make her fortune," he said.

"Doing what?" I said.

"Marrying well," he said.

"Starting with you?"

"I suppose," Washburn said. "One achieves, in some circles, a certain, ah, tone, I guess. Also, in addition to my academic earnings, there is a considerable trust fund. My father was aggressive in banking."

"Prestige and money," I said. "Good start."

"Yes."

"Love?" I said.

"She was not unkind," Washburn said.

# 23

*I had a drink* at the bar in Lock-Ober with the Special Agent in Charge at the Boston FBI office. He was a smallish guy with glasses, and he didn't look like much of a crime fighter. Which often worked for him. His name was Epstein.

"You on the kidnapping deal on the south coast?" I said.

"Heidi Bradshaw's daughter," Epstein said. "Yeah, we're on it, too."

"Know anything Healy doesn't?"

"Nope, we're sharing."

"That's so sweet," I said.

"We try," Epstein said, and sipped some

bourbon. "People aren't liking federal agencies much these days."

"Is it because we're being governed by a collection of nincompoops?" I said.

Epstein grinned at me.

"Yeah," he said. "Pretty much."

"It'll pass," I said. "We got through Nixon."

"I know," Epstein said. "You got anything for me?"

"Heidi Bradshaw's birth name was probably Hilda Gretsky," I said. "She might have been born in 1959 in Dayton, Ohio."

"Busy, busy," Epstein said.

"I got nothing else to do," I said.

Epstein nodded.

"You been out there?" he said.

"Dayton? Not yet. I was hoping maybe you could enlist one of your colleagues out there to run it down."

"Where'd you get your information?" Epstein said.

"Heidi's first husband, a professor at Lydia Hall College in New York."

"Name?"

"J. Taylor Washburn."

Epstein nodded. He didn't write anything down, but I knew everything was filed.

"Yeah," he said. "We'll run that down for you."

"Thanks," I said.

"It's our case, too," Epstein said. "She go to Lydia Hall?"

"No," I said. "But I suspect she has claimed to."

"Some reinvention going on?" Epstein said.

"It's the American way," I said.

"Sure," Epstein said. "You told Healy this?"

"Yeah, but we both figured your resources in the Dayton area were better than his."

"Or yours," Epstein said.

"Much better than mine," I said.

"You were there," Epstein said, "at the wedding when the whole thing went down."

"Yep."

"Why?"

"Her story is that she was at the moment between husbands and needed an adequate substitute for the wedding," I said.

"So if, say, the wine wasn't chilled, she could ask you to fix it?"

"I guess."

"You believe her?"

"No."

"There are women like that," Epstein said. "I'm Jewish, I know a lot of them."

"Isn't that anti-Semitic?" I said.

"Only female Semites," Epstein said.

"You've not had good fortune with the women of your kind?" I said.

"Or any other," he said.

"So it's more misogyny," I said.

"You're right," he said. "I was imprecise. Anybody paying you on this case?"

"I'm looking into it on my own," I said.

"Because they kidnapped somebody on your watch," Epstein said. "So to speak."

"Something like that. I wasn't very useful."

"You were looking out for Susan," Epstein said. "That's useful."

"How do you know?" I said.

"Because she was there. Because I am a skilled investigator. And because I know what you're like."

"Didn't do the kidnap victim much good," I said.

"What I hear, no one could. If you had

it to do over again, would you do it different?"

"No," I said.

Epstein grinned.

"That's right," he said. "You wouldn't."

# 24

*Peter Van Meer* lived in a very big condo-
minium on top of the Four Seasons, with
a view of the Public Garden and eternity.
I had a long time to study eternity because Van Meer kept me waiting for at
least twenty minutes in the room where
the maid left me. It was a big room with
heavy furniture and leather-bound books.
Many of the books had Latin titles and
looked as if they had been printed in the
nineteenth century. Van Meer probably
called the room his study. Everything was
expensive and perfectly matched and
color-coordinated, and arranged, and ap-

propriate, and as warm as a display room in Bloomingdale's.

I turned from the window when he came in.

He said, "Sorry to keep you waiting, my man."

He put out his hand as he walked toward me.

"Pete Van Meer," he said.

He was a large man with a big, square face, gray hair, and a swell tan. He wore a black shirt with several buttons undone, and a black watch plaid sport coat over pearl-gray slacks. We shook hands and I sat down in a dark brown leather armchair on the far side of a low mahogany coffee table with fat curved legs. Van Meer stood beside his desk.

"Drink?" Van Meer said.

"No, thanks," I said.

Van Meer grinned.

"Don't mind if I do," he said.

He went to a sideboard, which concealed a refrigerator, and made himself a tall Courvoisier and soda. He brought it back with him and sat on the edge of his desk. He made a faint toasting gesture toward me and took a pull.

"First of the day," he said.

"Always the best," I said. "You were married to Heidi Washburn."

He smiled down at me happily.

"Man," he said. "What a ride that was."

"Tell me about it," I said.

He took another pull.

"She could fuck the hinges off a firehouse door," Van Meer said.

"Good to know," I said.

"Oh, momma," he said, and drank some more cognac.

"How'd you meet?" I said.

"My wife at the time, Megan, was a big patron of the arts, you know? I was with her at some gallery reception for some whack job that threw paint on his canvas, you know?"

"I sort of like paintings where a horse looks like a horse, or at least reminds me of a horse," I said.

"You and me both, brother," Van Meer said. "Anyway, my wife at the time, Megan, is taking this dildo around, and introducing him to the guests, and I'm trying to gag down enough white wine to get me through the evening, and I look around and I'm standing beside this firecracker of a broad. You seen her?"

"I have," I said.

"Then you know what I mean," Van Meer said. "So she looks at me and says, 'You bored?' And I say, 'Not a big enough word for what I am,' and she goes, 'Do you like white wine?' And I say, 'No.' And she says, 'Me, either. Let's get out of here and get a real drink.' So we did."

"When was this?"

"Nineteen eighty-two," he said.

"She still married to Washburn?" I said.

"The art professor, yeah."

"Adelaide was born in 1985?" I said.

He nodded.

"You having any luck finding her?" he said.

"I've not found her yet," I said.

"But you will."

"Yes," I said. "I will."

He went to the sideboard and made himself another drink.

"I'm a lush," he said. "But a jolly one."

He drank some of his cognac and soda. His face darkened.

"And I love my daughter."

I nodded.

"I'm sorry," I said. "But I need to ask if you're sure she's yours."

His face stayed dark.

"We never DNAed her," Van Meer said.

He sipped his drink.

"You know," he said. "Even if we DNAed her now, and she turned out to be Washburn's or something? It wouldn't matter. She's my daughter."

His eyes were wet-looking. I thought he might cry.

"Do you think she's alive," he said.

"Have you heard from the kidnappers?" I said.

"No."

"There's no reason to do such an elaborate kidnapping and then kill her," I said. "She's alive."

"What do they want?" Van Meer said.

"I don't know yet."

"I have tons of money," Van Meer said.

"Can't hurt," I said.

"I can hire you to find her," Van Meer said. "Any amount, doesn't matter."

"No need," I said. "I'm looking for her now."

"If you need anything, anything that money can buy, just say so. It's yours."

"I'll keep it in mind," I said. "How long did the marriage last?"

"Me and Heidi? We got divorced when Adelaide was five."

"Nineteen ninety," I said.

"Yes."

"Why did you get divorced?"

Van Meer took a slow drink and shrugged.

"Bradshaw," he said.

"She was having an affair with him."

"Yeah, sure. I mean that wasn't such a big deal. She'd fooled around before. Hell, so did I. All during the marriage. We both did. But Bradshaw . . ."

He finished his drink and went to the sideboard and refreshed the glass.

"She was too far into Bradshaw," he said. "She stopped coming home. Stopped having sex. Stopped being fun. When she was with you, Heidi could be a big lot of fun."

He stayed at the sideboard holding his drink.

"Divorce contentious?" I said.

"No. I liked her. Hell, I probably loved her."

"Generous settlement?" I said.

"Oh, sure," he said. "I set up a big trust fund for Adelaide. She's set for life. And Heidi got a lump-sum settlement instead of alimony. It was how she wanted it. Alimony would have stopped as soon as she married Bradshaw."

"Ever meet Bradshaw?" I said.

"No."

"Know anything about him?"

"No," Van Meer said. "Heidi never talked about him. Never said a word."

"Who asked for the divorce?"

"Her," Van Meer said. "Told me she was in love with Bradshaw and wanted a divorce so she could marry him."

"And he was the one she'd been seeing?"

"I assume so."

"But you don't know," I said. "You didn't put a private eye on her or anything?"

"No," he said. "But I can tell you there was someone. On the rare occasions in that period when she would consent to sex, I knew. I don't know how. I just knew I wasn't the first one of the day. You know?"

I nodded.

"Do you know Heidi's birth name?" I said.

"No."

"Do you know where she's originally from?"

He shook his head. He was looking past me now, out across the Public Garden, at the slow rise of Beacon Hill.

"Why would someone take Adelaide?" he said. "And not ask me for money?"

I had no answer for him. Which was all right, I guess, because I don't think he was asking me. He took a drink. There were tears on his face. He kept studying the view out his expensive window.

"I want to know why that is," he said.

## 25

*Epstein came into my office* on the day before Halloween and sat down, put his feet on the edge of my desk, and tilted his chair back.

"Hilda Gretsky was in fact born in Dayton," he said. "She attended Stebbins High School but didn't graduate, went to beautician school and didn't finish, worked at a bookstore called Books & Co. for a couple years, and headed for New York, looking, I assume, for Mr. Right."

"That's where he usually is," I said.

"I'll mention it to my daughters," Epstein said.

"You have daughters?"

"Three."

"Wife?" I said.

"Not currently," Epstein said.

"Anything else interesting about Heidi?" I said.

"People at the bookstore say she wasn't much of a bookseller. Said she spent most of her time reading the books," Epstein said.

"That's it?" I said.

"Yep. No record. Nobody much remembers her."

"Parents?"

"Deceased," Epstein said.

"Siblings?"

"None."

"Boyfriends?" I said.

"None that we could find," Epstein said. "We have located her current husband."

"From whom she's estranged."

"Yeah."

"Healy gave me an address in Padanarum, on the south coast," I said.

"That's one," Epstein said. "He's got houses in London and Tuscany, too."

"What's he do?"

"Seems to be some sort of consultant for the Information Agency."

"That doesn't support three houses."

"Probably not," Epstein said.

"So," I said. "He's got money, too."

"Apparently."

"What a coincidence," I said. "All her husbands have been rich."

"Lucky her," Epstein said.

"Where's Bradshaw now?" I said.

"Padanarum, last we checked," Epstein said.

"How did he make his money?"

"The old-fashioned way," Epstein said. "His father earned it."

"What's he do with the Information Agency?" I said.

"Information adviser."

"Propaganda?" I said.

"We don't do propaganda," Epstein said. "Our enemies disseminate propaganda. We provide information."

"It's good to be us," I said.

"Used to be," Epstein said.

"Is that subversive?" I said.

Epstein shook his head and didn't answer.

"Is it a civil service job?"

"Nope," Epstein said. "I don't think so. I

think it's a campaign contribution at the right time to the right guy's job."

"He work regularly?"

"He consults from time to time," Epstein said.

"How long they been separated?" I said.

"Year and a half," Epstein said.

He balanced easily on the hind legs of the chair. He seemed confident that he wouldn't go over backward.

"Know anything about the current escort?" I said. "Guy named Clark."

"I know you knocked him on his ass," Epstein said.

"Piece of cake," I said. "What's his last name?"

"Morrissey," Epstein said. "Clark Morrissey. Competed for a while as a bodybuilder. Male stripper. Bouncer at some upscale clubs. Probably where she met him."

"Can't fight a lick," I said.

"Most folks can't," Epstein said. "But people like Heidi Bradshaw don't know that."

"And he looks good," I said.

"That's what I been getting by on," Epstein said.

## 26

*There was something* a little serpentine about Harden Bradshaw. He was tall and smooth, with a smallish head and dark eyes. His eyelids drooped. His movements were very supple. His handshake was languid. His hand was cold. We talked in a glassed-in section of the wraparound veranda of his home, looking across the marsh grass and the sand at the ocean. He was wearing a black turtleneck sweater and a camel-colored corduroy sport coat with the collar turned up.

"What's your relationship with Mrs. Bradshaw?" I said.

"Separated."

"There's separation that leads to divorce," I said. "And sometimes, separation that leads to reconciliation. Which are you?"

"It is what it is," Bradshaw said. "I am hoping for reconciliation."

"What is the, ah, presenting syndrome for the separation?" I said.

Bradshaw looked at me.

"You been shrunk?" he said.

"In a manner of speaking," I said.

"What's that mean," Bradshaw said.

"I often get to sleep with a shrink," I said.

"Ah, the woman you brought to Tashtego," he said.

"Yes."

"Perhaps if you had paid less attention to her," Bradshaw said. "You might have been more helpful to Heidi."

"Perhaps," I said. "I didn't see you there."

"I was supposed to be. At the last minute I simply couldn't go. Couldn't stand the civilized pretense, you know?"

A middle-aged golden retriever pushed her way in through the flap on the doggie door and came to my chair. She sniffed me carefully, accepted a scratch behind her ear, then went and lay in a patch of sunlight on the floor. There was no rug. And the chairs we were sitting in were most of the furniture in the glass room.

"Any other men involved?" I said.

"With Heidi, there are always men involved," he said. "The separation is not, however, about that."

"What is it about?"

"We each need time to discover ourselves," Bradshaw said.

"Getting help?" I said.

"I am seeing a therapist," Bradshaw said. "I don't know what Heidi is doing."

"Spend much time in Washington?"

"Information Agency?" he said. "Some. I spend some time overseas as well."

"Where?"

"Middle East, Central Europe," he said. "London."

"Before you were separated, did Heidi go with you?"

"Sometimes," he said.

Through the archway behind us I could see that the living room looked sort of empty, too. It had a rug and a couch, but not much else.

"Ever meet a guy named Rugar?" I said.

"No, why do you ask?"

"You're the first person in this deal that might have," I said.

"Because of my government service?"

"He's been in government service, too," I said.

"Is he the kidnapper?"

"Yes."

"And you're suggesting I might be complicit?"

"Somebody had to have access to Rugar."

"Perhaps you are complicit," Bradshaw said. "You certainly did nothing to stop the kidnapping."

"I wish I were," I said. "Then I could tell myself what I want to know."

"I see no reason to be flip," he said.

"Any reason will do," I said. "Have you ever been involved in covert operations?"

"For God's sake, I'm a PR adviser. I know nothing about covert."

"And if you did, you wouldn't admit it," I said. "Because then it would no longer be covert."

Bradshaw smiled a pale smile.

"I assume spies do not go about telling people they are spies," he said.

"So the fact that you deny it is meaning-less," I said.

"I suppose so," Bradshaw said.

"Did you get along with Adelaide Van Meer?" I said.

"Heidi's daughter?" He shrugged. "I thought she was spoiled and childish and somewhat neurasthenic. But we didn't fight or anything."

"Did Heidi know you thought that about her daughter?"

"Hell," Bradshaw said. "She thought that, too, except it was her daughter, and she was sort of required to love her."

# 27

*Susan's idea of a great Chinese meal* is a small bowl of brown rice and some chopsticks. But occasionally she indulges my taste for something more exotic, and goes with me to P. F. Chang's in Park Square, where she nibbles at her rice and watches in understated horror as I wolf down some sweet-and-sour pork. We were doing that on a quiet Tuesday evening, when the Gray Man came to our table and stood.

Susan's face tightened.

I said, "Care to join us?"

"I would," he said, and pulled out a chair and sat.

The waitress came over.

"Would you like to see a menu?" she said.

"No. Bring me Stoli and soda," the Gray Man said. "A double."

She went for the drink. The Gray Man looked at Susan.

"Dr. Silverman," he said.

Susan nodded once without speaking. I gestured at my sweet-and-sour pork.

"Bite?" I said.

He shook his head.

"I'm not here for trouble," he said.

"The management will probably be pleased," I said.

The waitress brought him his drink. He took some in.

"I would like you to stop looking into the events at Tashtego Island," he said.

"How come?" I said.

"We have a history, you and I, and it has caused me to hold you in some regard," he said.

"Aw, hell," I said.

"I do not wish to kill you," he said.

"He likes me," I said to Susan. "He really, really likes me."

"You are, as usual, flippant. And you

are, as usual, involved in something you don't understand," Rugar said. "Nothing is as it seems."

"The old illusion-and-reality issue," I said. "You're a heavy guy, Rugar."

He gestured to our waitress for another drink.

"I will not," he said, looking at Susan, "do any harm to Dr. Silverman. It would compromise the adversarial dignity of our history."

The waitress set Rugar's drink down before him and took his empty glass and left.

"You believe me?" Rugar said.

"Your word is good," I said.

"Yes," he said. "It is. And I give you my word that you are blundering about in a situation that you don't understand."

"That's a description of my whole professional life, Rugar."

He nodded and drank some vodka.

"The world would be less interesting," Rugar said, "without you in it. The valid adversary. The worthy opponent. The one who keeps me sharp."

"But . . ." I said.

"But your present course will lead us to

a point where you are intolerable," Rugar said.

"And?" I said.

"And I will kill you," Rugar said.

"You tried that already," I said.

"And would have succeeded if you had been other than who you are. I should have made sure."

"You should have," I said.

"I don't make many mistakes," Rugar said, "and I never make one twice."

"You ever run into Harden Bradshaw?" I said.

He looked silently at Susan for a moment.

Then he said, "Perhaps if you spoke with him."

Susan shook her head.

"You think you know him," she said.

"Very well," Rugar said.

"And you think if you threaten him he will walk away from this?"

"I am hopeful," Rugar said, "that he might recognize how much easier life would be if he just enjoyed it with you and didn't have to keep an eye out always for me."

"He might recognize it," Susan said. "He won't do it."

Rugar looked at me.

"On the other hand, I have nothing to lose by trying," Rugar said. "He won't strike first."

"You're sure?" Susan said.

"Yes. Unless I threaten you, which I have said I won't do," Rugar said.

"You think he would kill you if you threatened me?"

"He would try," Rugar said.

Susan looked at me.

"Would you?"

"I'd succeed," I said.

Rugar almost smiled.

"I will not harm Dr. Silverman," he said, and stood.

"But I fear I will have to deal with you."

I nodded.

"You will," I said.

He picked up his glass, drained it, put it down, and walked away. I returned to my sweet-and-sour pork. Susan looked after him for a while.

"It's almost as if you liked each other," she said.

"We almost do," I said.

"Is his word, in fact, good?" Susan said.

"Yes," I said. "He won't bother you."

"You know that."

"Yes."

"I'm not asking for reassurance," Susan said. "I believe you. But how do you know?"

"Rugar's a professional killer, pretty much willing to do anything. Unless he has some rules for himself, he has no limits, and he's in free-float. There's no tether."

"So he makes some up."

"Yep."

"Do you do that?"

"Don't need to," I said. "I have you."

When we were through eating, I signaled for the check.

"The gentleman in the gray suit has taken care of your dinner," the waitress said.

"Did he give you a credit card?" I said.

"No," she said. "Cash. Quite a lot. He said to keep the leftover as a tip."

I nodded. The waitress left. I smiled.

"Even in his grand gesture," I said, "he's leaving no paper trail."

"And even accepting the grand gesture," Susan said, "you're looking for a paper trail."

The valet brought my car. We got in and started down Charles Street.

"He probably frightened you," I said. "Maybe you should stay the night with me and I'll comfort you."

"Comfort?" Susan said. "Is that what you're calling it?"

"Yes," I said.

# 28

*On an overcast morning* with the temperature in the high thirties, Hawk, carrying a shoulder bag and wearing jeans with a black muscle shirt, came into my office and poured himself some coffee.

"No jacket?" I said. "It's November."

Hawk flexed a biceps.

"You got the guns," Hawk said. "You put off the winter sleeves long as you can."

"Where's the piece?" I said.

"What make you think I'm packing," Hawk said.

"Hawk, for crissake, you haven't gone

anywhere without a gun since you were a pickaninny."

"Pickaninny?" Hawk said.

"I value tradition," I said.

Hawk grinned and opened his shoulder bag and took out a huge, silver .44 Mag with a bone handle.

"Case we get assaulted by a polar bear," he said.

"Good to be ready," I said.

"Understand the Gray Man after you again."

"He is," I said.

"Why don't we just kill him," Hawk said.

"Can't," I said.

Hawk shrugged.

"No harm to ask," Hawk said.

"No."

"Susan says it be about the business on Tashtego," Hawk said.

"It be," I said.

"Would you be, by chance, mocking my authentic ghetto dialect?" Hawk said in his Laurence Olivier voice.

"No," I said. "I be down with it."

"Love when honkies be trying to talk black," Hawk said. "It's like a guy in drag."

"You in on this now?" I said.

"Yep."

"Because Susan called and said so?" I said.

"Yep."

"Any other reason?"

Hawk grinned.

"Don't want to lose the only guy left in the world who uses the word *pickaninny*," he said.

"Okay, lemme fill you in a little."

We went through a second pot of coffee as I told Hawk what I knew, which didn't take long, and what I didn't, which was extensive.

"And so you been doing what you do, which is to poke around in the hornet's nest until you irritate a hornet," Hawk said.

"Yes."

"Not a bad technique," Hawk said, "long as you got me to walk behind you."

"And it has the added pleasure of being annoying."

"Yes," Hawk said. "That a plus."

"Any thoughts?" I said.

"It's not enough that I am the world's deadliest human being?" Hawk said. "You asking me to think, too?"

"Or whatever it is you do," I said.

"Well, maybe it ain't a kidnapping," Hawk said. "No ransom request."

"That we know of," I said.

"A visit from the Gray Man? Telling you to buzz off? You know a lot of kidnappers make house calls?"

"Doesn't mean it isn't a kidnapping," I said.

"He wanted a simple kidnapping for money, he didn't have to put together an army complete with helicopters."

"He got away with it," I said.

"So far," Hawk said. "But he lucky, and he good. No way a pro like Rugar going to choose that kind of a setup to kidnap somebody."

"Somebody chose it," I said.

"Maybe it's something else, and the kidnapping is a head fake," Hawk said.

"What something else would it be?"

"How many people got killed?"

"Six by Rugar," I said. "One by me."

"Maybe that be the plan," Hawk said.

"A murder disguised as a kidnapping?" I said.

"Like you haven't thought of what I'm saying."

"I have," I said. "I'm just being devil's advocate."

"Nobody better," Hawk said.

"It's still awful amateurish," I said. "I can't see Rugar doing it that way."

"You saw him do it," Hawk said. "And seven people died, counting the one you killed. That's what we got for facts."

"And if it's not a kidnapping," I said, "then maybe we can start thinking of this as a murder case and start looking for motive."

"We don't have to decide," Hawk said. "We can look into all possibilities."

"Probably can exclude the guy that went over the cliff," I said.

"We know the motive there," Hawk said. "And we can at least drop the security guys to the bottom of the list."

"It's not quite a fact," I said. "But it's a pretty good bet that the thing was an inside job."

"And it a pretty good bet that somebody knew how to get hold of Rugar."

"So it might be smart to look for a guy who knew the island, and might have a connection to Rugar," I said.

"Got anybody in mind?"

"It's not much, but Bradshaw knows the

island, he used to own it, and he has worked overseas for the government."

"Doing what?" Hawk said.

"Information officer," I said.

"Things are not," Hawk said, "always as they seem."

"True," I said.

"So we look into Bradshaw, and we also see if we can find someone who would want to kill the minister or the groom," Hawk said.

"Still a big order for a two-man unit," I said.

"Yeah, but the two men," Hawk said, "be us."

# 29

*Hawk and I met Ives* at the bar in the Seaport Hotel on a Friday night. The hotel was an easy walk from the federal courthouse, where Ives had a desk. He was sandy-haired and tweedy, with a blue oxford shirt and a rep-stripe tie.

"Ah, Lochinvar," Ives said, "and his raptor friend."

"How about the end of the bar," I said.

We sat on the first three bar stools, Ives between me and Hawk. "I assume you are seeking information," Ives said, "to which you have no legal right, and for which you have no clearance."

"Exactly," I said.

"And you are planning to pay for the drinks."

"I am," I said.

Ives smiled and ordered Johnnie Walker Blue on the rocks. I had the same thing with soda. Hawk ordered champagne.

"We don't sell Krug by the glass, sir," the bartender said. "I can give you a list of what we do serve."

"I'll have a bottle," Hawk said.

"I assume you wish to discuss our mutual friend the Gray Man," Ives said.

"You know what I'm involved in?"

"Tashtego," Ives said.

"Pretty good," I said.

"I'm a listener," Ives said. "It is my profession."

"He still working with you guys?"

"Mr. Gray has joined the private sector."

"No more money from his uncle?" I said.

"Not to my knowledge."

"So who pays him now?" I said.

"I don't know," Ives said.

"Can you find out?" I said.

Ives smiled and sipped some scotch.

"Probably," he said.

"Have any idea what he's been doing recently?"

"Other than Tashtego? No."

"Can you find that out?" I said.

"Probably," he said.

Hawk was silently drinking champagne, alert to every movement of a young woman in a tight black dress at the end of the bar. You could never be sure where danger lay. I had typed up a list of salient people in the Tashtego affair. I took the list from my inside pocket and placed it in front of Ives on the bar.

"Recognize any of the names?" I said.

Ives took some glasses from his breast pocket and studied the list.

"There are several names anyone would know," he said after a time. "Reubens, for instance. Everyone who loves music knows who he is. The Lessards are prominent residents of the Main Line. Of course, Peter Van Meer right here in Boston. Great wealth."

"You know what I'm after," I said. "Anyone who had a connection to Tashtego and would have the wherewithal to hire Rugar."

"Bradshaw," Ives said.

"What about him?"

"Government employee," Ives said.

"Information adviser, I'm told."

Ives smiled.

"Aren't we all," he said.

"He with you guys?"

Ives didn't answer.

"What can you tell me about him?" I said.

"Nothing," Ives said.

"If you were me," I said, "would you look into him?"

"Yes," Ives said.

"Anyplace you'd start?"

Ives shrugged. He finished his scotch, put the glass on the bar, and stood.

"That's it?" I said. "That's what I get for buying you Johnnie Walker Blue?"

"It's a lot for one shot of scotch," Ives said.

"Do you know how much the stuff costs?" I said.

Ives shrugged slightly and walked out of the bar.

Still looking at the woman in the black dress, Hawk said, "Bradshaw."

"You were listening."

"Sort of," Hawk said. "Babe in the black dress might be a security risk."

"You think we should frisk her?"

"We? I was thinking I frisk her while you fight the boyfriend."

I looked down the bar. The woman in the black dress was sitting with an out-sized young man jammed into an expensive suit, who looked, by himself, like an offensive line.

"Good deal for me," I said.

"I could fight the boyfriend and you could frisk her," Hawk said. "But what's she get out of that?"

"Her loss," I said.

Hawk nodded.

"What you gonna do 'bout Bradshaw?" he said.

"I think I'll look into him," I said.

"'Stead of fighting the boyfriend?"

"Yeah."

Hawk shook his head sadly.

"All work and no play . . ." he said.

# 30

*We were walking up the mall* in the center of Commonwealth Ave toward Kenmore.

"You see them?" Hawk said.

"Black Caddie?" I said. "Double-parked just past Dartmouth Street. Outbound side?"

"And?" Hawk said.

"Gray Ford double-parked just this side of Exeter, inbound side?"

"Whaddya think," Hawk said.

"Could be nothing," I said.

"Or it could be something," Hawk said.

"We probably need to decide," I said, "before we get between them."

"Be my guess," Hawk said.

The cross streets were alphabetical: Arlington, Berkeley, and so on. We were at the corner of Clarendon.

"If they don't plan to shoot us, we look foolish taking evasive action."

"True," Hawk said.

"But," I said. "Say they do want to shoot us."

"We don't want to encourage that," Hawk said.

"You know my motto," I said. "Better to take needless evasive action, at the risk of looking foolish, than not to, and look dead."

"That your motto?"

"I'm having it printed on my business cards," I said.

"We can turn the wrong way onto Dartmouth, and probably shake them in the alleys," Hawk said.

"But then we won't know who they were," I said. "Or if they were anybody."

"If they anybody, we know where they come from," Hawk said.

We had stopped walking and sat on a bench in the mall like a couple of tourists resting their feet. Neither of the cars moved.

"If they're Rugar," I said. "They won't care about you. They'll be after me."

"You right," Hawk said. "Maybe I just mosey on home."

"Maybe you just mosey on up Clarendon to the alley, and you run lickety-split up the alley and back down Exeter."

"Lickety-split," Hawk said.

"And I'll stroll languidly along toward Dartmouth, and if we time it right . . ."

"We'll time it right," Hawk said.

I nodded.

"We can end up with you behind the Exeter Street guys on that side. And I'm behind the Dartmouth Street guys on this side."

"They expecting to catch us between them," Hawk said, "and we catching them between us."

"Rugar won't be one of them," I said. "Even if he sent them."

"Why not?"

"He would do it alone," I said.

Hawk nodded.

"One question," Hawk said. "We get them surrounded, then what?"

"Then we'll see," I said.

"You just a planning fool," Hawk said.

# 31

*We crossed Clarendon Street and paused,* as if we were looking at the kids playing in the small park. Then for the benefit of the guys in the cars, Hawk shook hands with me. He turned up Clarendon toward Newbury Street. I gave him a little wave. As he passed the public alley halfway to Newbury, out of sight from either car, he turned down. I turned right and left the mall to walk along the sidewalk, past the little park, on the river side of Commonwealth. I tilted my head as if I were listening, and then took out my cell phone and stopped and flipped it open and pretended to answer it.

"'Twas brillig,'" I said into the dead phone, "'And the slithy toves . . .'" I nodded. "'Did gyre and gimble in the wabe . . .'" I nodded again and listened and nodded. "'All mimsy,'" I said, "'were the borogroves.'"

Then I closed the phone and put it back in my pocket. Hawk was quick. He should be about at Exeter Street by now. I began to saunter along toward the Ford. I could feel the weight of my Browning on my right hip. There were fourteen rounds in the magazine, and one in the chamber. On each side of Commonwealth there was a march of brick and brownstone town houses. Most had small yards with shrubs. Halfway up the block toward Dartmouth I paused, staring, as if I'd seen something on the front walk of a town house. I stepped in and crouched down for a closer look, and as I did so, shielded by a shrub, I took the Browning off my hip and cocked it. Then I stood, with the gun against my right thigh, concealed in the skirt of my topcoat, and continued toward Dartmouth. It was getting dark. But in the streetlight at the corner of Exeter, I saw Hawk appear. Just before I came up on the Ford, I could see two men get out of the Caddie a block up on the other side. My guys would wait until I passed. I could see the car windows were down. They might not get out. They might shoot me from the car. I was whistling "Midnight Sun" as I strolled along. Footloose in the Back Bay, looking for love and feeling groovy. As I got to the car, I took a fast shuffle sideways, and standing just behind the passenger window, I pointed my gun in the window and said, "Move and I'll kill you."

The guy on my side had a sawed-off shotgun in his lap. He was right-handed, and it was too awkward for him to point it back at me. Sadly, he tried anyway and I killed him. The driver slammed the car into reverse and spun his wheels. I jumped away and steadied my aim on him. He slammed the car into drive and spun his wheels, getting away from the curb. The smell of burnt rubber was strong. He careened up Commonwealth. I aimed carefully at the back of the car and didn't shoot. There were other cars. There were people. I could probably hit the car, but I wouldn't stop it without shooting him. Which, given the circumstance, was uncertain. He was no use to me dead anyway. One was enough. The car ran the red light at Dartmouth Street, and slammed a right and disappeared with the disapproving sound of horns beeping angrily behind him. I looked across Commonwealth at the corner of Dartmouth. The black Caddie was still there. Hawk was sitting on the hood. I didn't see anyone else. I made a palms-up gesture at Hawk. Where are they? Hawk jerked a thumb toward the sidewalk on the other side of the car. I holstered my gun and walked across.

# 32

*I sat with Quirk in an* interrogation room in the new police headquarters, across the table from the two guys Hawk had collared. One had a big, rapidly discoloring bruise on his right cheekbone. The other guy had a bandage across his forehead. Hawk had apparently banged him face-first against the edge of the Cadillac roof. Beside them sat a smallish man with a lot of curly hair that stood straight out from his head. He had on a blue work shirt and a wrinkled sport coat in a small gray-green check.

"Hawk clean on this?" I said to Quirk.

Quirk grinned.

"Good Samaritan," he said. "Saw what was going down and intervened. We're crediting him with a citizen's arrest."

I nodded.

"They got a lawyer?" I said.

"Don't seem to speak much English," Quirk said. "Not sure they know they can have a lawyer."

"Where they from?" I said.

"I don't know, one of those *stan* countries in Central Asia," Quirk said. "Boogaloo-*stan*, or something."

I looked at the two guys. They were ordinary-looking guys. Both had dark hair. One had a beard touched with gray. He wasn't that old. Whiskers always seem to be the first to go.

There was a knock and the interrogation-room door opened.

"Captain," a woman said, "lawyer's here for these two."

A black man came into the room wearing a gray three-piece suit that looked vaguely as if it might have been made for him in Europe. His close-cut hair was gray.

He wore gold-rimmed glasses and carried a briefcase.

"Lamar Dillard," he said. "I represent these two gentlemen."

"You're not some guy from the pool," Quirk said. "You cost money. Who hired you?"

"An interested third party," Dillard said, "who I am under no obligation to name."

Quirk nodded.

With Dillard was a small woman with smooth black hair worn long, and big, dark eyes. She wore a plain gray dress with a white collar, and low shoes that were probably comfortable.

"This is Ms. Glas," Dillard said. "Ms. Glas will translate."

"You know me," Quirk said. "This is Spenser."

Ms. Glas went to the two shooters and began to murmur softly to them in a language that didn't sound familiar.

"Yes, Captain, I do know you," Dillard said. "Is Mr. Spenser a police officer."

"Mr. Spenser is the intended victim," Quirk said.

"If there was a crime intended," Dillard said.

"We know they were driving a stolen car with phony plates," Quirk said. "We know they had concealed weapons for which they are not carrying any proof of licensing. They might even turn out to be undocumented aliens."

Ms. Glas continued to speak softly to the undocumented aliens. They looked at Dillard and said something to Ms. Glas. She shook her head and spoke some more.

"And of which of these alleged crimes is Mr. Spenser the alleged victim?" Dillard said.

"They tried to kill him," Quirk said.

"From their appearance, the opposite would seem the case," Dillard said. "Ms. Glas, ask them if their injuries came from being mistreated by the police?"

She spoke. They answered.

"They say it is a black man who did that, on the street," Ms. Glas said.

Dillard grimaced slightly.

He said to Quirk, "Could you excuse us, Captain. I think I need to speak to my clients alone."

"We'll be in my office," Quirk said. "The officer can direct you."

"I know where your office is, Captain," Dillard said.

"Me, too," Quirk said, and we went out of the room.

# 33

In Quirk's office I said, "I don't care about these guys. I want to know who hired them."

"Yeah," Quirk said. He poured two cups of coffee and set mine in front of me on the edge of his desk. "Plus, we get into a trial and we may need Hawk to testify . . ."

"And Dillard might be able to raise questions about his respect for the law?"

"Something like that," Quirk said.

"Well, you have some bargaining chips," I said. "Probably no papers, stolen car, fake plates, unlicensed guns."

"Dillard may come up with papers," Quirk said, "and a couple gun licenses."

"What police chief in the state would issue a carry license to these two clowns?" I said.

Quirk looked at me silently.

"Oh," I said, "chicanery."

"There are towns in this great commonwealth," Quirk said, "where you can buy a gun license, if you know the right name to whisper."

"And Dillard would know the right names."

"Works for Tony Marcus a lot," Quirk said. "Hell, Ty-Bop's got a gun license."

"From where?"

"Some Podunk town out in western Mass," Quirk said.

"Ty-Bop's never been west of Brighton," I said.

"I'm sure he hasn't," Quirk said. "Tony's got a white lawyer, too, guy named Stackpole. Got a suit just like Dillard's. Tony uses him for white specialty stuff."

"You think Tony sent Dillard?"

"Whether he sent him or not, Tony knows he's here," Quirk said. "And he don't disapprove."

I nodded.

"I wonder what Tony would have to do with two guys from Whatzistan," I said.

"Nothing legal," Quirk said.

"Maybe we'll find out," I said.

"We won't get anything on Tony," Quirk said. "One of Dillard's jobs, if Tony's involved, is to make sure Tony don't get mentioned."

"Language barrier doesn't help," I said.

"No, it doesn't," Quirk said. "I got a call in to Epstein, see if he can find us somebody."

"I wonder where Ms. Glas is from," I said.

"We'll find out," Quirk said. "Before the ADA gets here, you got anything you want to tell me about why two immigrant gunnies want to kill you?"

"Why would anyone?" I said.

"Hard to imagine," Quirk said. "You think it's got anything to do with Tashtego?"

"You know I'm still involved with that?" I said.

"I keep track of you," Quirk said. "For my scrapbook."

"Might be Tashtego," I said. "You remember the Gray Man."

"Yep."

"He might have become annoyed."

"What I know about the Gray Man," Quirk said, "he'd have done it himself."

"Yeah," I said. "That bothers me a little, too."

# 34

*It was nearly an hour before* Dillard came into Quirk's office and sat down beside me, facing Quirk.

"Ms. Glas is with my clients," Dillard said. "They were confused when I asked them earlier, language problems, all that. They now say that their injuries were the result of police abuse."

"Wow," Quirk said. "They were confused."

"How would you like to handle this?"

"The police abuse? I got ten independent witnesses to confirm the street altercation where they received the injuries."

"Who was the black man in that altercation," Dillard said.

"An interested third party," Quirk said.

"When we get to trial, I can compel you to reveal his name," Dillard said.

"Uh-huh."

"If we get to trial," Dillard said.

"Uh-huh."

A heavy young woman with short black hair and a strong nose reached in to knock on the open door to Quirk's office. She had large horn-rimmed glasses, and a gray pant suit that didn't fit very well.

"Come in, Esther," Quirk said.

"Hello, Martin," she said, and looked at Dillard. "How are you, Lamar?"

She put her hand out to me.

"I'm Esther Gold," she said. "I'm the ADA on this case."

I gave her my name.

"You the complainant?" she said.

"I guess so," I said.

She looked at Quirk.

"Spenser has worked with us in the past," Quirk said. "I've asked him to sit in."

Esther nodded.

"Lamar, you're representing the two

guys whose names I can't pronounce?"
she said.

"I am," Dillard said.

"So let's talk," she said.

"Mr. Dillard," Quirk said, "was just questioning if we had to proceed to trial with these guys."

"What would be our alternative?" Esther said.

She rummaged in her bag as she spoke and came out with a Kleenex and wiped her nose. She sounded like she might have a cold. She looked around for someplace to throw the Kleenex and found nowhere and stuffed it back in her bag.

"I don't know," Dillard said. "But it's something we might explore. All lawyers would rather go to trial, Esther, you know that."

"I do," Esther said. "Go ahead. Explore."

Dillard leaned back a bit in his chair, rested his elbows on the arms of the chair, placed the tips of his fingers together in front of him, and rested his chin on them.

"They are part of a four-man crew," Dillard said, "here for reasons not germane to our concerns. The leader of the crew was in the car that escaped the shootout.

They fear he may have been the passenger, now presumably dead. He was the one who spoke English, and it was he who negotiated the contract on Mr. Spenser. They were told that the name of the man who put the contract out was Rugar. He was described to them as dressing all in gray. Apparently, they found it amusing."

Dillard paused.

"That's it?" Esther said.

"They have no record, they have committed no serious crime."

"Other than conspiracy to murder," Esther said. "Possession of an unlicensed firearm, illegal immigration."

Dillard opened his briefcase and took out a manila envelope.

"Gun permits and immigration papers," Dillard said. "They were fearful and hid them for fear the police would confiscate them."

Quirk looked at me. I grinned. Esther saw it.

"Captain?" she said.

"How long ago did you fill in the names?" Quirk said.

"Captain," Dillard said. "Your work has soured you."

Quirk nodded.

"It has," Quirk said.

"Okay," Esther said, "you represent two little lambs lost in a strange place. What can they do for me?"

"They've given you the man who hired them," Dillard said. "They will testify."

Esther nodded.

"I'm sure they'd make compelling witnesses," she said.

"As would the, ah, Good Samaritan who assaulted them," Dillard said. "Whose identity I believe I know."

Esther looked at Quirk. Quirk nodded his head toward the door.

He said, "Let's you and me confer privately, Esther."

They stood.

As he left the office, Quirk jerked his head at Dillard and said to me, "Don't let him steal any paper clips."

When we were alone, I said to Dillard, "Seen Tony lately?"

"Tony?"

"Tony Marcus," I said. "You represent him, don't you?"

"Sometimes," Dillard said. "You know Tony, do you?"

"Yep," I said. "Helped send him up once."

Dillard nodded without speaking.

"Why would Tony Marcus's expensive mouthpiece be interested in a couple of goons from Itty-bitty-stan?" I said.

"Tony is not my only client," Dillard said.

"You got any that Tony disapproves of?" I said.

"The implication is insulting," Dillard said.

"Good," I said. "You want to have a duel?"

"Why do you wish to insult me?" Dillard said. Very dignified.

"I think Tony's gotten himself involved in all of this somehow," I said, "and your job is to get him uninvolved. If that means getting the two goons off, fine. If it means throwing them off the back of the sled, fine. Nobody knows what they actually said to you except your translator and maybe you."

"You are, of course, free to speculate," Dillard said.

"Thanks," I said.

Quirk came back into his office with Esther.

"We'll keep them," Esther said.

Dillard said, "That's disappointing, Esther."

Esther smiled.

"And I feel really bad about it," she said. "But we thought it might be nice to have our own translator talk with them, you know? Some sort of investigation before we let go of them."

"Arraignment?" Dillard said.

"Someone from my office will call you," Esther said. "Let you know."

"It should be prompt," Dillard said.

"Of course it should," Esther said.

"Very well," Dillard said. "I'll need to talk with my clients, explain their situation."

"Feel free," Esther said. "I'll walk you back."

Esther said good-bye to Quirk, nodded at me, and followed Dillard out of the office.

"Gee," I said, "Lamar didn't say good-bye to either one of us."

"Not a friendly guy," Quirk said.

I nodded.

"Rugar worked with me up in Marshport a while back," I said. "Tony Marcus was in that mix. In fact, he lent us a guy named Leonard . . ."

"I know Leonard," Quirk said.

"So Leonard worked with Rugar," I said.

"Which means Rugar and Tony have a connection," Quirk said. "Maybe we can roll them both up."

"Think big," I said.

"That's what my wife always says."

"Wishful thinking," I said. "You're Irish."

"Jesus," Quirk said. "The secret's out."

# 35

*Pearl was visiting in my office,* as she often did when Susan was busy all day and out in the evening. When Healy came in he saw her on the couch and paused to pat her. She wagged her tail but didn't get off the couch.

"Bring Your Dog to Work Day?" Healy said.

"I get so lonely," I said.

"We got a ransom demand," Healy said. "For Adelaide Van Meer."

"Who got it, her mother?"

"Yep. Five million dollars."

"Note," Healy said. "Block letters, looks

like someone printed them with their off hand."

"Payoff instructions?"

"To come," Healy said.

He took a photocopy of a letter from his inside pocket and smoothed it out on my desktop in front of me.

**IF YOU WANT YOUR DAUGHTER BACK COME UP WITH $5 MILLION. YOU HAVE A WEEK TO GET IT. WE'LL CONTACT YOU THEN.**

"How'd it arrive?" I said.

"By ordinary mail, according to her," Healy said. "She 'thoughtlessly disposed' of the envelope before she realized it was important. No return address. Postmarked, she thinks, in Boston."

"She going to pay?"

"Yes. Says she is going to talk with Adelaide's father about it."

"You told her that paying was no guarantee she'd see her daughter."

"I did," Healy said. "I also told her that not paying was no guarantee of seeing her daughter."

I stood up. Pearl raised her head. A

walk was possible. A cookie? I walked across the room and patted her.

"She share any other thoughts with you?" I said.

"None worth repeating," Healy said. "She's 'horribly worried' about her daughter."

I nodded. Pearl realized the pat was all she was getting, and put her head back down on the couch. I walked back to my desk and stood and looked out the window.

"Whaddya think?" I said to Healy.

"I think it's bullshit," Healy said.

"Took them an awful long time to send the ransom note," I said.

"Might be a wacko," Healy said. "Might be some harebrain who had nothing to do with the kidnapping."

"Along for the ride," I said. "Thinks he can score a little cash from somebody else's crime."

"It happens," Healy said.

"I know. You think it's one of those?"

"They usually show up sooner than this, also," Healy said.

"Yeah," I said. "They do."

"You got a theory?" Healy said.

"The ransom's an afterthought," I said.

"What kind of a kidnapping has the ransom as an afterthought?" Healy said.

"One not about the ransom," I said.

"Most not-ransom kidnappings are about child custody," Healy said. "Or sexual perversion, or another kind of ransom."

"Give us the plans to the atom bomb or you'll never see your daughter again," I said.

"Something like that."

"None of those seem to be in play here," I said.

"No. This seems like something being made up as they go along," Healy said. "You know this guy, Rugar. That his style?"

"No."

"Some people took a run at you, and bungled it."

"You know about that," I said.

"I'm a trained investigator," Healy said. "That Rugar's style?"

"No."

"But it was Rugar did the kidnapping," Healy said.

"I saw him do it," I said.

"Maybe that's what you were there for?"

"You think?" I said.

"I don't think," Healy said. "I guess. If I knew something, maybe I could think."

"If I was there for a purpose related to the kidnapping, then it would mean that Heidi knew it would happen," I said. "She's the one who hired me."

"So?"

"So if she is, your theory of the crime is that she had six people killed, including her new son-in-law, and her daughter kidnapped, and hired me to be there so I could watch."

"It's a theory," Healy said.

"Motive?" I said.

"Picky, picky," Healy said.

We were quiet. I realized I didn't know what I was looking at out the window. I turned from the window and sat back down at my desk.

"Suppose the son-in-law had a will?" I said.

"Of course he did. People in that bracket, they have wills and trusts and pre-nups and post-nups and up-nups . . ."

"Be nice we could see the pre-nup and the will," I said.

Healy was quiet for a time, looking at the thought.

"Wouldn't do any harm," he said. "But even if it is for money, the very late ransom demand makes no sense."

"So maybe it's time to unleash the forensic accountants," I said. "Can you do that?"

"I am a captain in the Massachusetts State Police," Healy said.

"I'll take that for a yes," I said.

Healy grinned.

"Tallyho!" he said.

# 36

*Despite that it was November,* Susan and I spent two days at a resort in Rhode Island, in a big cottage on the beach. The cottage had a fireplace and a king-sized bed, and in the late afternoon of the first day we were lying on the bed, with the fire burning, looking at the ocean. It was a clear blue day, just starting to darken, and the pre-winter ocean looked gray and hard as it rolled up onto the smooth sand where the seabirds hopped about.

"'Roll on,'" I said, "'thou deep and dark blue ocean, roll. Ten thousand fleets sail over thee in vain.'"

"Is that Byron?" Susan said.

"Maybe," I said.

Outside our picture window, the sea-birds were very busy at the edge of the waves, scooting back and forth as the waves came in and broke and spread out on the beach. I assumed they were looking for things edible that the waves had roiled up. But I never did know for sure, and when I brought the question up to Susan, she trivialized it. I got up and added wood to the fire and came back and re-propped my pillow and lay on the bed beside her.

"Are we just going to lie on the bed all afternoon and look at the ocean?" Susan said.

"We can look at the fire, too," I said.

"That's it?"

"Except for occasional outbursts of scandalous sexuality," I said.

"Oh," Susan said.

She stood up and took off her tank top, and unsnapped her bra and let it slide down her arms.

"Do you feel such an outburst approaching?" I said.

"I fear that I'm in its grasp," Susan said.

She unzipped her skirt and dropped it to the floor and stepped out of it, and wiggled out of her fairly exotic underpants.

"Would you experience it as depravity," I said, "if I suggested that you leave the high heels on?"

"I would," she said.

"But?" I said.

"I admire depravity," she said.

"Does this mean I should disrobe?" I said.

"Yes," Susan said.

So I did. And when I was done, Susan smiled, gave me a thumbs-up, and jumped on me. Then, for a while, the rest was silence . . . of a sort.

By the time we were finished it had gotten dark, and the ocean was visible mostly as the white foam of the beached waves showed in the moonlight. As soon as we were through making love, Susan squirmed under the covers and pulled them up to her chin.

"Um," she said.

"I couldn't agree more," I said.

"We left the shades open," Susan said.

"So we did," I said.

"What if someone had passed by?"

"Might have been instructive for them," I said.

We lay quietly for a time. Only the ocean moved in the darkness outside our window. My gun was on the bedside table.

Susan looked at it.

"There it is," she said.

"My gun?" I said.

"Our constant companion," Susan said.

"Better to have it and not need it . . ." I said.

"I know," Susan said. "I know all that."

"Part of the business," I said.

"I know that, too," Susan said.

"You have a gun," I said.

"Yes," Susan said.

"You'd use it if you had to," I said.

"I would."

We lay quietly, listening to the ocean.

After a while, I said, "I believe the cocktail hour is upon us."

"In a minute," Susan said.

She rolled over against me and put her arms around me and pressed her face against my chest. We stayed that way for a time. Then Susan let go and rolled over and bounced out of bed.

"I'll be ready in ten minutes," she said.

"You will not," I said.

"Will too," she said.

It actually took her forty-eight minutes.
But it was well worth the wait.

# 37

*While I was examining* the well-dressed young women passing below me on Berkeley Street, the phone rang. Still looking out my window, I picked it up and said "Hello."

"I'm in Franklin Park," Quirk said to me on the phone. "Near White Stadium. You might want to drop by."

"Okay," I said, and hung up.

It was a very nice fall day, more October than November, and a lot of the people walking by were coatless. I watched one especially attractive woman walk across Boylston Street and into Louis's before I put on a leather jacket to cover my gun, and went downstairs to get my car.

It was easy to find Quirk. I could have probably located him from an orbiting spacecraft. There were half a dozen cruisers, some with the lights still rotating, at least two unmarked police cars, an ambulance, the coroner's truck, yellow tape, flashbulbs, an amplitude of gawkers, and a couple of television news trucks at the edge of the scene. A uniformed cop stopped me after I parked behind one of the TV trucks and got out.

"Crime scene, bud," he said. "Got business here?"

"Quirk asked me to come by," I said.

The cop nodded and turned and yelled.

"Captain?"

Quirk looked over, saw me, nodded his head, and gestured me toward him. The patrolman who had stopped me grinned, and gestured me in with a big sweep while he pretended to lift a velvet rope.

"Right this way, sir."

I walked over to Quirk, who was standing with a detective I didn't know, looking down at a body covered with a tarp.

"Know anybody named Leonard Rezendes?" Quirk said.

"Know a Leonard works for Tony Marcus," I said. "Don't think I ever knew his last name."

Quirk nodded.

"He's had several. But Rezendes is what's on his driver's license."

Quirk bent down and turned back the tarp. It was hard to be sure because his head had been shot up pretty good, but it seemed to be the Leonard I knew.

"I think that's him," I said.

"It is," Quirk said. "Some kids called nine-one-one couple hours ago."

"They around?" I said.

"They wouldn't give a name, and there was no one here when we arrived," Quirk said. "I got a guy canvassing the crowd."

"Doesn't appear to be accidental," I said.

"Wow!" said Quirk.

"I'm a detective," I said. "It comes pretty easy."

"At least four rounds to the head," Quirk said. "Probably forties. We found four shell casings."

"So he was done here."

"Unless they brought the casings and threw them around to fool us," Quirk said.

"Boy, you must be a detective, too," I said.

"And a captain," Quirk said. "Lot of blood on the ground."

"Hard to fake that," I said.

"Yeah," Quirk said, and grinned. "We assume he was killed here."

"See?" I said.

"Leonard was Rugar's connection to Tony," Quirk said.

"Yes."

"You think it got him killed?"

"Something did," I said.

"His wallet's still in his pants," Quirk said. "Seven hundred dollars. His Rolex is still there; somebody told me it was worth about twenty thousand dollars."

"For a watch?" I said.

Quirk shrugged.

"Wasn't a robbery," Quirk said.

"Four in the back of the head," I said. "Sounds like an execution."

"Any other thoughts?" Quirk said. "You being a detective and all."

"Rugar killed him to break his connection

to the attempt on me," I said. "Or maybe Leonard did it without Tony, and it's Tony's way of explaining to him how wrong that was."

"And breaking the connection to him," Quirk said, "in the process."

"True," I said.

"It's still all speculation," Quirk said.

"At least," I said, "we're starting to have things to speculate about."

"Which is what we do," Quirk said.

"Until we know something," I said.

"Which we will," Quirk said.

# 38

*Hawk and I were working out* at the Harbor Health Club, which was becoming accessible again as the Big Dig went out not with a bang but a whimper. Even though the place was now more upscale than Buckingham Palace, Henry Cimoli, who ran the place, still kept a small boxing room in back as some sort of gesture toward us, or maybe to his roots.

"Susan say you going out too much by yourself," Hawk said as he worked on the uppercut bag.

"I figure they might let things slide a little after the last shot at me went so bad."

"Rugar don't let nothing slide," Hawk said.

"This has been atypical Rugar," I said, "since they started playing 'Here Comes the Bride' on Tashtego Island."

"Maybe stuff we don't know," Hawk said.

"That's for sure," I said.

I was throwing hooks at the heavy bag. *Body, body, head, head.*

"I mean maybe he got problems distracting him, why he farmed the hit out on you," Hawk said.

"He doesn't normally do that," I said. "Sees it as being dependent on other people, I think."

"You ever think it a fuckup?" Hawk said.

"Tashtego?"

Hawk nodded.

"Didn't go the way it was supposed to," Hawk said. "And Rugar be scrambling ever since?"

"Well, it sure isn't vintage Rugar," I said.

Martin Quirk came into the boxing room. He nodded at Hawk. Hawk nodded back.

To me, Quirk said, "I need you to look at another body."

"Everybody's got to be good at something," I said to Hawk.

"Looking at bodies?" Hawk said.

"It's a gift," I said.

I untaped my hands, put a leather jacket on over my sweats, put my gun in a side pocket of the jacket. Small gun today, five-shot .38 with a two-inch barrel. Strictly defensive.

"You probably safe with the captain," Hawk said. "I meet you here when you through?"

"I'll bring him back," Quirk said.

Hawk nodded and went back to the uppercut bag. I followed Quirk out to the street, where his car was illegally parked at the curb, impeding traffic. With a callous disregard for anyone else driving at the time, Quirk drove us swiftly to Boston City Hospital, where I was able to look at the distorted corpse of a man I may have killed.

"Found him by the Charles River Dam," Quirk said, "bumping around the lock."

"Pretty sure it's him," I said. "I only saw him for a minute, and he's been in the water for a while."

"No ID," Quirk said. "No DNA match in

the database. They're trying to lift some fingerprints, but he's pretty waterlogged."

"You get a slug out of him?"

"His head," Quirk said.

I nodded.

"We'll go over to the lab," I said. "I'll fire a test round for you. If the slugs match, it's him."

"The driver probably dumped him soon as he cleared from you," Quirk said.

"Which would put him in the river somewhere this side of the BU bridge," I said.

"And the river brought him down."

"Surprising no one spotted him," I said.

"Might have been under for a while till he started to puff up," Quirk said.

I nodded.

"Nice," I said.

Quirk gestured with his head, and the morgue attendant slid the drawer shut.

"Come on," Quirk said. "I'll buy you lunch."

"What could be better," I said.

There was a sandwich shop up Albany Street a little where Quirk bought sandwiches and coffee for us. I declined the sandwich and drank the coffee while we sat in Quirk's car and watched the activity at the wholesale flower market across the street.

Without looking at me Quirk said, "And the two goons got shanked."

"My goons?" I said. "That tried to kill me?"

"Yep. In the jail yard, yesterday. Guard found them both in a corner. Throats cut."

"Jesus Christ," I said.

"Yeah," Quirk said. "Last man standing."

"Tony got to them," I said.

"Or Rugar," Quirk said. "Pretty sure it was an inmate or a guard."

"What a pleasure to watch a trained mind work," I said.

"Years on the job," Quirk said.

"Anybody talk to them, before their demise?"

Quirk shook his head.

"Epstein finally found us a translator," Quirk said. "He and I were scheduled to interview them today."

"What a coincidence," I said. "Was their attorney going to be present?"

"Yep."

"Good old Lamar," I said. "Murder weapon?"

Quirk shrugged.

"Maybe a utility-knife blade," Quirk said. "We're looking into it."

"What do you expect to discover?"

"Zip," Quirk said.

"Any suspects?"

"Everybody," Quirk said. "You got yourself into something pretty ugly."

"Yeah, but at least I'm not making any progress," I said.

"Assuming it's all related to Tashtego," Quirk said, "I count eleven people killed so far. Two of them by you."

"I know," I said.

"For what?" Quirk said.

"I don't know," I said.

"Me neither," Quirk said.

"Don't feel bad," I said. "Epstein and Healy don't know, either."

Quirk finished his sandwich and carefully wiped his mouth on a paper napkin.

"The funny thing is," he said, "we know who did the original crime. But we don't know why, and we can't find him."

"Yet," I said.

"Hawk walking around with you?"

"Most of the time," I said.

"I was you," Quirk said, "I'd make it all the time."

"Yeah," I said. "Nobody in this deal seems to mind killing people."

"And you are probably a sentimental favorite to be next," Quirk said.

"Would you miss me?" I said.

"No," Quirk said.

# 39

*The guy in the morgue* had in fact been killed with a bullet from my gun. So we sort of knew who he was. Of course, we still didn't have a name for him. Every time we learned something, it wasn't enough. According to Rule 4 in *Spenser's Detecting for Dummies*, if you aren't getting anywhere and you don't know what to do, go annoy somebody. So Hawk and I went off to annoy Tony Marcus.

Ty-Bop and Junior were in evidence. Ty-Bop was the shooter, a skinny kid wearing a watch cap pulled way down over his ears. He seemed to be listening to something the rest of us couldn't hear, and moving to its beat. Junior was the muscle, vast and thick and stolid.

Hawk lounged at the bar near Ty-Bop. Ty-Bop would kill anything that Tony pointed him toward. But that aside, he always seemed to admire Hawk. He never said anything, but he watched him all the time, the way a schoolyard player would watch Michael Jordan.

Junior brought me into Tony's office and patted me down.

"Got a gun, Tony," Junior said.

"Let him keep it," Tony said. "I just want to know he's not wearing a wire."

"Nope," Junior said. "No wire."

Tony gestured him out, and Junior closed the door behind him as he left.

"Gives us a little more room," I said.

Tony smiled.

"He's a big one," Tony said.

"Sorry about Leonard," I said.

"Uh-huh."

"How's your daughter," I said.

"No worse," Tony said.

"Still with . . ."

"No," Tony said.

I nodded. Tony waited.

"We've known each other for a while," I said.

"Uh-huh."

Tony was beautifully dressed in a brown tweed jacket with a light-blue windowpane pattern. He had on a blue shirt and a brown silk tie.

"We've done each other some favors," I said.

"Uh-huh," Tony said. "'Specially the time you got me sent to jail."

"We were much younger," I said.

"Everyone was," Tony said. "You helped me out with my kid, couple years ago."

"I did," I said.

"You know I'm not wired. Anything we say in here is off the record and doesn't leave this office," I said. "I'm not after you."

Tony smiled faintly.

"Oh, good," he said.

"You remember Rugar," I said.

"He was with you in Marshport," Tony said.

"As was Leonard," I said.

Tony took out a slim cigar and snipped the end and lit it carefully with a silver desk lighter.

"Rugar was involved in a big-deal kid-

napping on Tashtego Island a while back,"
I said. "I was there."

"Heard about that," Tony said.

"So here's a theory I'm working on," I
said. "I've been pecking away at the
Tashtego thing since it went down. Somewhere along the way I got too close; I wish
I knew where. And Rugar decides I have
to go. But for whatever reason, he doesn't
want to do it himself, so he remembers
Leonard from Marshport, and he asks
Leonard to take care of it for him. Probably
for a good price."

Tony took the cigar from his mouth and
looked at the lit end, seemed satisfied with
the way it was burning, and put the cigar
back in his mouth.

"But Leonard doesn't do it himself," I
said. "Instead, he hires these guys from
Far Goofystan, and they botch it."

Tony let out a soft puff of smoke. I always like the smell of a good cigar.

"And Leonard panics," I said. "He knows
he shouldn't have gone around you and he
doesn't know what else to do, so he tells
you. You know that the trail will eventually
lead back to you unless you take action.
So you send Lamar down to see what

these guys are likely to do, and get them out if he can. And you kill Leonard to underscore his fecklessness. Lamar can't get these guys out, but he explains their language limitations, and that so far he's the only one can talk with them. So you got a couple days. You use the time to make arrangements, and when Quirk and Epstein schedule an interview with their own interpreter, Lamar gives you the news and you have the two goons killed."

"Fecklessness," Tony said.

"It is also my theory that you got nothing to do with Tashtego except that Leonard dragged your name in."

Tony blew some more cigar smoke around.

"Fecklessness," he said. "I like it. Fecklessness."

I waited.

"The theory makes sense," Tony said after a while.

"Anything I might have missed," I said.

"Nothing that matters," Tony said.

"And I shouldn't anticipate any problems from your, ah, organization," I said.

"Not if you are discreet," Tony said.

"Any idea where Leonard got these guys?"

"Might have been a guy he met up in Marshport," Tony said. "There was some Afghani influence, wasn't there?"

"Boots Podolak was in business with an Afghani warlord named Haji Haroon," I said.

"It wouldn't be feckless," Tony said, "to think there could be a connection with Leonard."

"Worth looking into?" I said.

"Dead end," Tony said. "Somebody aced Leonard's only contact up there."

"Could that someone be Ty-Bop?" I said.

"The boy gets restless," Tony said. "Trust me, there's no loose ends up there."

"So," I said, "you got this buttoned up pretty tight."

"I didn't initiate this. I wouldn't have permitted it. I don't need any of this. It interferes with business."

"So you closed it down."

Tony nodded.

"Except for Lamar," I said. "That's how I got to you."

"Lamar is my attorney," Tony said.

"And," I said, "being your attorney, he can invoke privilege whenever he needs to."

"And will," Tony said.

# 40

*It was the way it was* supposed to be in Boston in November. Gray and kind of chilly and a steady rain falling. Cars had their headlights on at ten in the morning when Hawk and I drove to Epstein's office in Government Center.

"I be out here by the elevators," Hawk said. "I not going in any FBI office."

"J. Edgar's ghost will be grateful," I said.

"You think it wearing a dress?" Hawk said.

I went in. Epstein pushed a folder across the desk at me as I sat down.

"Been working with our forensic accounting folks," Epstein said.

"The excitement never stops," I said.

"You can learn a lot from accountants," Epstein said.

"I have no doubt," I said. "What'd you learn?"

"Van Meer and Bradshaw are both nearly broke," Epstein said.

"Can Heidi take credit for that?"

"She costs both of them a sickening amount of money," Epstein said. "Van Meer didn't help himself much by being a drunk and slopping through most of his inheritance. Bradshaw pays a huge alimony, and he still maintains that private island. Essentially, since they've split, for her."

"Tashtego," I said.

"Yep. He was never as rich as Van Meer in the first place, though from the looks of what he spent, he tried to pretend he was. If it was to impress her, then she pretty well cleaned him out."

"That college professor was lucky to escape with his life," I said.

"Her first husband, yeah. Other than sort of a modest income from what investments he still has working for him," Epstein said, "Bradshaw's biggest asset is a very large life insurance policy with Heidi as beneficiary."

"I were Bradshaw," I said, "that might make me nervous. How about Van Meer."

"He cashed his in for the surrender value," Epstein said.

"So he's not worth much to them dead or alive," I said.

"The bank is moving to foreclose on his condo," Epstein said.

"When you talk with him, he seems to have not a care in the world," I said. "Except maybe he still misses Heidi."

"He's a drunk," Epstein said. "Drunks are good at denial."

"Have to be, I suppose," I said. "How about the pre-nup and stuff."

"Pre-nup, Lessard's will," Epstein said. "It's all in there in more detail than you'd ever want. From the moment of marriage, Adelaide and Maurice became each other's primary heir. And no matter what the family does later, each is entitled to the estate as it existed at the time of marriage."

"And the Lessard lawyers bought that?" I said.

"Lawyers can only do what the client will agree to," Epstein said. "Far as I can see, the Lessards thought they were marrying up. They probably thought the arrangement was in their favor."

I picked up the folder. It was thick. I put it down.

"You suppose," I said, "all this, helicopters, and shoot-outs, and assassination attempts, and kidnapping, and FBI and state cops, and Boston cops, and a lot of people dying . . . you suppose it's all about fund-raising?"

Epstein shrugged.

"What is it usually about?" Epstein said. "Any crime?"

"Love or money," I said.

"Or both," Epstein said.

# 41

*I met Ives on the little bridge* over the Swan Boat Pond in the Public Garden. It was rainy again, and Ives was under a colorful golf umbrella. I was wearing my leather jacket and my Boston Braves cap (circa 1948). Umbrellas are for sissies.

"You called?" I said.

Even though there was no one within twenty yards of us, Ives softened his voice when he answered. Maybe you had to have a heightened sense of drama to be a spook.

"The Gray Man," Ives said, "was in our employ in Bucharest in the early 1980s."

It was too late in the year for swan boats. They were put away. But the ducks were still here, and they cruised the pond hopefully.

"He was probably fun-loving and carefree in those days," I said.

"Mr. Bradshaw was, at that time, at the American embassy in Bucharest."

"Small world," I said.

"It gets smaller," Ives said. "In 1984 Mrs. Van Meer visited Bradshaw in Bucharest."

"Heidi Van Meer?" I said. "Now Heidi Bradshaw?"

"Yes."

"In 1984 she was married to Peter Van Meer," I said.

Ives shrugged. We were silent as two very dressed-up women strolled past us. We both watched them as they passed and for a time afterward.

"You think they might be enemy agents?" I said, as Ives stared after them.

"No," Ives said. "The woman on the right, I was admiring her ass."

"Discriminating," I said. "I was admiring both."

"My dear Lochinvar," Ives said. "I went to Yale."

"And never recovered," I said. "So we have Heidi, Bradshaw, and Rugar all in Bucharest in 1984. Rugar and Bradshaw both working for the Yankee dollar."

"And Mrs. Van Meer, involved romantically with Bradshaw."

"Any concrete connection," I said, "between Rugar and Bradshaw?"

"They worked out of the same building," Ives said. "Beyond that I don't know, and can't find out."

"Even though you went to Yale?" I said.

Ives smiled.

"All of us," he said, "went to Yale, Lochinvar."

"I know," I said. "Why aren't there any spooks from, say, Gonzaga, or Florida State?"

"Imponderable," Ives said.

"How long was Heidi in Bucharest?" I said.

"Don't know," Ives said. "Mr. Bradshaw was there through 1986."

"Rugar?"

"Don't know."

"Is he working for you now?" I said.

"No."

"You know who he is working for?" I said.

"To my knowledge Mr. Rugar is not currently working for anyone."

Below us a small vee of ducks paddled industriously under the bridge in the fond possibility that there'd be peanuts.

"Anything else?" I said.

"No, I appear to have emptied the purse," Ives said.

"I appreciate it."

Ives nodded his head to accept my thanks.

"We both live in worlds where the cynicism is age-old and millennium-deep," Ives said. "We are both cynical, and with good reason. But you are not just cynical, Lochinvar. I find it refreshing."

"How about you," I said. "Are you just cynical?"

"Yes," Ives said.

We both smiled and were quiet, and watched the ducks for a while before Ives went his way and I went mine.

# 42

*Hawk joined us* for Thanksgiving dinner at my place.

"Have we had Thanksgiving together before?" Susan said.

"Can't recall it," Hawk said.

"Why on earth not," Susan said.

"Most holidays nobody trying to shoot him," Hawk said. "Which seem kinda strange to me, too."

"Does that mean that you are often alone on Thanksgiving?" Susan said.

Hawk smiled.

"No, Missy," he said. "It don't."

Hawk and Susan were drinking vintage

Krug champagne, which Hawk had contributed, at the kitchen counter. Pearl was deeply into the couch in front of the fire. There was a football game on the tube, with the sound off, in deference to Susan, and I was cooking.

"What's for dinner?" Hawk said.

"I thought I'd experiment with roast turkey this year," I said.

"Nice choice," Susan said.

"Stuffing?" Hawk said.

"Yep, and cranberry sauce."

"Clever additions," Susan said.

"Paul with his girlfriend?" Susan asked.

"Yes, in Chicago. They said they were going to stay home and cook for each other."

"Eek!" Susan said.

"He living out there now?" Hawk said.

"Yes. They're both with a theater company."

I opened the oven and pulled out the oven rack with the turkey on it. I basted the turkey with a mixture of applejack and orange juice.

"How will you know when it's done," Susan said.

"Cook's intuition," I said, and shoved the

turkey back into the oven and closed the door.

"Plus the little red plastic thing in the turkey," Hawk said, "that pops up when it's ready."

"Big mouth," I said to Hawk.

"It's all right," Susan said. "I love you anyway."

"How come?" Hawk said.

"Damned if I know," Susan said.

Thanksgiving at Spenser's: Hawk and Susan sipping champagne, Pearl asleep in front of the fire, the rich scent of the roasting bird filling the room, the dining room table set and beautified by Susan, Hawk's shotgun leaning on the corner of my bookcase.

When I got the food to the table my duties were over. Hawk carved surgically. Susan served meticulously. I ate. Pearl watched each mouthful closely. Susan had ruled that it was absolutely forbidden to feed her from the table. All three of us ignored the rule.

"Wonder what Rugar doing for Thanksgiving," Hawk said.

"And Adelaide," I said.

"No," Susan said. "Not on Thanksgiving.

On Thanksgiving we worry about whether we'll be hungry enough before bedtime to have a turkey-and-stuffing sandwich with cranberry sauce and mayo."

"No business?" I said.

"None," Susan said.

"No concern for the less fortunate?" I said.

"Fuck 'em," Susan said.

"That be my other Thanksgivings," Hawk said.

"Works for me," I said. "Pleasant and not fattening."

"I was using a metaphor," Susan said.

"Fact it probably burn calories," Hawk said.

"Today is a day to enjoy the fact that we love each other," Susan said. "That's enough."

"All three of us?" Hawk said.

"And Pearl," Susan said.

"'Scuse me," Hawk said. "All four of us?"

"You know we love you, Hawk," Susan said. "Pearl included. And you damned well know that in your own singular way, you love us."

Hawk grinned widely.

"Singular," I said.

"Sho 'nuff, Missy," Hawk said to Susan.

He bent over and gave Pearl a bite of turkey. He watched her chew it, still bending over, and when she was finished she looked up at him hopefully.

"Sho 'nuff," he said to her.

# 43

*I went to see Van Meer.* We sat in the same room we'd sat in last time. He offered me a drink. I declined. He made one for himself. It appeared that he'd started early today. He was already a little glassy-eyed at two in the afternoon.

I couldn't think of a way to ease in, so I just went.

"You in financial difficulty?" I said.

"No," he said, "not at all."

"The bank's foreclosing on this place," I said.

"Oh, the banks are always doing something," he said. "I don't pay any attention."

"You've cashed out your life insurance," I said.

Van Meer smiled happily.

"Had better things to do with it," he said.

"What about your daughter? She was the beneficiary."

"She was marrying into one of the richest families in the country," he said. "She didn't need it."

I nodded. I wondered if he remembered that his daughter was missing.

"So the reports of your financial vulnerability are greatly exaggerated."

Van Meer nodded several times.

"You bet," he said. "I'm rich."

"In the early 1980s," I said, "while she was married to you, Heidi was in Bucharest, Romania, with Harden Bradshaw."

"I know," Van Meer said.

"Talk about that," I said.

"We had a big fight," he said. "She went to Bucharest. When she came back, we made up. In fact, that's when Adelaide was conceived."

He sipped his drink. He was sedate. No guzzling.

"What was the fight about?"

"Oh, God," he said. "I don't know. We had fights all the time."

"You know she was cheating on you?"

"Yes."

"With Bradshaw?"

"Yes."

"Might it have been a fight about that?" I said.

"Coulda been," Van Meer said.

"How'd you feel about that?" I said.

Van Meer shrugged.

"Hell, she cheated on me all the time, with anybody available," he said, and sipped again.

"How'd you feel about that?" I said.

He laughed.

"You sound like all of my many shrinks," he said. "Why do you want to know all this?"

"If I knew ahead of time what was important to know and what was not . . ." I said.

He nodded.

"Yeah," he said. "I can see that."

He had another swallow. Like a lot of experienced boozers, he could go a long time before he began to slur his words. He held his glass up a little and looked at his drink.

"Not too long after we got married, we had some wiring done at our new house," he said. "She fucked the electrician."

I nodded.

"She needed sex, and she needed variety," Van Meer said. "She was fucking me while she was married to that art professor. She was fucking Bradshaw when she was married to me."

"Busy," I said.

"Yeah."

"Looking for Mr. Right?" I said.

"Mr. Feels Good," Van Meer said. "As far as I could tell, she fucked plumbers and limo drivers and delivery men, and for all I know doctors, lawyers, and Indian chiefs."

"One man would never be enough," I said.

"That is correct."

"And you could live with that?" I said.

"Better than I could live without her," Van Meer said.

"And now you have to do both," I said.

Van Meer nodded and took another sip.

"Yup," he said.

# 44

*It was the Thursday* after Thanksgiving, the last day of November, with a gentle but persistent rain falling all along the south coast. In Padanarum, Hawk waited in the car for me while I went up on the porch and rang the bell for Harden Bradshaw. I could hear the surf from the waterfront side of the house. I could smell wood smoke, and when Bradshaw opened the door, I could look past him and see the fire burning on the big hearth in his living room.

"You again," he said.

"Glad to see you, too," I said. "May I come in?"

"What do you want?"

"Several things," I said. "Like where your stepdaughter attended college."

"She went to Penn for two years before she dropped out," Bradshaw said. "Before that she went to Miss McGowan's School in Ashfield, western Mass," he said.

"Prep school?"

Bradshaw nodded.

"For young ladies," he said.

He sounded a little scornful.

"Why'd she drop out of college?" I said.

"You'll have to ask her mother," Bradshaw said. "Is that all?"

"Can we discuss you and Heidi in Bucharest in 1984," I said.

"I have nothing further to say to you," Bradshaw said, still blocking the doorway. He had on a plaid flannel shirt today, and wide-wale corduroy pants.

"I wonder if she might have met a man named Rugar while she was there."

"I don't know," Bradshaw said. "I had nothing to do with the events at Tashtego. I have no idea where my stepdaughter is. I don't know anything about this Rugar fellow, and I am quite frankly tired of you."

"Then you'll be tired of dreaming," I said.

"Excuse me?"

"Allusion to a song," I said. "I could sing it all for you."

"I do not find you amusing," Bradshaw said.

"What a shame," I said. "So you probably don't want me to sing, either."

"I believe we're through here," Bradshaw said.

"Before you go," I said, "lemme tell you what I think. You and Rugar were working out of the American embassy in Bucharest. I think you knew Rugar from there. I think maybe Heidi met him there as well."

"The American embassy in Bucharest is not a ma-and-pa store," Bradshaw said. "Many people worked there. I didn't know most of them."

"And yet nearly twenty-five years later, Rugar shows up at your wife's home and kidnaps your stepdaughter," I said. "Is it really that small a world?"

"For the record, Tashtego belongs to me," Bradshaw said.

Then he closed the door in my face and I heard the dead bolt turn. Some people have no sense of humor.

# 45

*Miss McGowan's School* was on top of a hill in western Massachusetts. It occupied all of a big old Civil War–era estate in Ashfield. Which is not too far from Deerfield, where there had been a massacre once. It was, as far as I could tell, the last excitement they'd had out there.

Hawk parked his Jaguar in front of the main building near a sign that said *Administration*.

"You be safe in there without me?" Hawk said.

"No," I said. "But you better wait here anyway; I don't want you scaring the girls."

"I keep doing this," Hawk said, "I going to get me one of those dandy-looking chauffeur's hats."

"I been hoping," I said, and got out of the car.

The building was probably the original statehouse, with a big porch that wrapped around three sides, and in the autumn sunshine offered a splendid view of the countryside. If you like countryside.

The headmistress was a tall, slim woman who looked a little like Charles de Gaulle. Her name was Isabel Baxter.

"A private detective," she said. "How utterly fascinating."

"Yes," I said.

"Do you carry a, ah, a gat?" she said.

"I wouldn't risk the McGowan School without one," I said.

She laughed. Sort of a high, fluty laugh, but genuine.

"Tell me what you can," I said, "about Adelaide Van Meer."

"The girl who's missing," Ms. Baxter said. "Heidi Bradshaw's daughter."

"Yes."

"Are you trying to find her?" Ms. Baxter said.

"Yes."

"The poor girl," she said.

I waited. Ms. Baxter thought about it. The way she was thinking told me there was something to learn, if she'd tell me. I began to assemble my every charm, the smile, the twinkle in the eye, the manly profile, maybe even a little flex of my biceps, if I could sneak it in. She wouldn't have a chance. I would lay it all on her like a tsunami, should she hesitate.

"I went to the McGowan School," Ms. Baxter said. "When I graduated, I went on to Mount Holyoke. When I graduated from Mount Holyoke, I came back here to teach French. After a time I became dean of students. After another while I became headmistress. I have spent nearly all my life here. I care deeply about the school."

"I can see why you would," I said.

She was going someplace, and I wanted to let her go there.

"But a school isn't buildings, or even headmistresses," she said, and smiled slightly at herself. "A school is the girls who come here, and flourish, and move on to college and careers and marriage, and when they have daughters they send them here and the school continues, organically, almost like a living thing."

I nodded. I'd had no such experience with schools, but it was touching to see someone who had. Even if it was illusory.

"So," she said, "to shortchange the children in order to preserve the school is oxymoronic."

I made no comment. She wasn't really talking to me anyway.

"Adelaide did not flourish here," Ms. Baxter said. "In her second year she took too many sleeping pills and nearly succeeded in killing herself."

"How old?" I said.

"Sixteen."

"What the hell was a sixteen-year-old girl doing with that many sleeping pills?" I said.

"She was a very troubled girl. We got her to the hospital and the school doctor arranged for her to see a local pediatrician. With the help of members of our board, we managed to allow the world to think it was an accident."

"But it wasn't," I said.

"No," Ms. Baxter said. "She tried to kill herself."

"Do you know why?" I said.

"I do not. Her mother came out to get her and brought her home, despite, I'm told, Dr. Weiss's objections. She never returned to school. Perhaps if you talked with Dr. Weiss."

"School doctor?" I said.

"No. Pediatrician. The school doctor, Dr. Feldman, never treated her, really. Just had her admitted to the hospital and arranged for Dr. Weiss to see her."

"Is he here in town?" I said.

"He is."

Ms. Baxter took a small piece of lavender-colored notepaper and wrote an address and handed me the paper.

"I'll be happy to call him for you," she said, "if you wish."

"Might be helpful," I said.

She nodded and stood, and went to her office door.

"Doris," she said to a secretary, "get Dr. Weiss for me, please."

Then she came back to her desk.

"After successfully covering up the attempted suicide," I said, "why did you decide to tell me now."

"The poor girl," Ms. Baxter said. "Now

she's been kidnapped, you are trying to find her. I had no right to withhold anything."

Her phone rang.

"Yes," she said, "thank you, Doris, put him on."

She spoke briefly on the phone to Dr. Weiss, made a note on her lavender notepaper.

"Three o'clock this afternoon," she said. "He will see you. Do you need directions to his office?"

"How many streets in this town?" I said.

"I believe five," Ms. Baxter said.

"I'll find him," I said. "I am, after all, a detective."

She smiled. I stood.

"I pray that you'll find her," Ms. Baxter said, and rose to walk me out. "And I hope you won't have to use your gat."

"Me, too," I said.

"Have you ever used it?" she said.

"Yes, ma'am," I said. "I have."

"Oh, dear," she said.

"Think how I feel," I said.

## 46

*Hawk pulled his Jag up* in front of the big white house where Dr. Weiss did business.

"You going to join me?" I said.

Hawk shook his head. I nodded and got out of the car.

"Y'all take yo' time, Miss Daisy," Hawk said. "I be waiting right here."

"Cute," I said, and walked up the flagstone path to the side of the house, where a self-effacing little sign said *Office*.

Weiss was a tall, thin guy with a gray crew cut and a jittery manner.

"At the behest of Dr. Feldman," Weiss

said, "I spoke with Miss Van Meer several times during her stay in the hospital."

"What can you tell me?" I said.

"Well, of course, this was some years ago."

"Five," I said.

Weiss nodded.

"She denied attempting suicide," he said. "Claimed it was an accidental overdose."

"You think?" I said.

"She accidentally took twenty sleeping pills?" Weiss said.

"Okay, so she tried to kill herself. Was she serious?"

"I don't know. She took all the pills she had," Weiss said.

"So maybe she was serious."

"Maybe," Weiss said.

"She was attempting to kill herself, or attempting to call attention to her circumstances," I said. "Either way, something's wrong."

"Yes," Weiss said.

"Do you know what?" I said.

Weiss leaned back a little in his chair.

"Shrinks hate questions like that," he said.

"Because?"

"Because we frequently don't know the answer," he said. "And we don't like not knowing."

"My sympathies," I said. "Can you guess?"

"We hate to guess, and in our practice we shouldn't guess, we should allow the patient to reveal his truth."

"I'm trying to find her," I said. "Maybe save her. I need any guesses you can give me."

"I know. I wish I could have worked with her, but her mother came and snatched her away as soon as she could leave the hospital."

"She needs work?" I said.

"In my judgment, she is a very unstable young woman," Weiss said.

"Can you amplify that for me?" I said.

"Do you know much about psychotherapy, Mr. Spenser?"

"Not enough," I said. "But I am the significant other of a shrink in Cambridge."

"Really. What is the shrink's name?"

"Nice," I said. "You framed the question gender-neutral."

Weiss smiled.

"We don't like to guess," he said.

"Susan Silverman," I said.

"I know her," Weiss said. "She's beautiful."

"Yes," I said.

"And very smart," Weiss said. "I've heard several of her papers."

"Yes."

Weiss seemed to lean back farther in his chair. I felt as if I had passed some sort of initiation.

"I truly don't know her issues," Weiss said. "But I've been in this line of work for a number of years, and my guesses are at least informed by experience."

"Never a bad thing," I said.

"Experience can inform," he said. "It can also distort."

"Sure," I said. "But inexperience is rarely useful."

He nodded thoughtfully.

"Well put," he said.

"Adelaide Van Meer?" I said.

He nodded.

"I believe she has been sexually molested," Weiss said.

"She say so?"

"No."

"More than once?" I said.

"Over a long period of time, I think."

"By whom?" I said.

"I don't know."

"What I know about sexual abuse," I said, "particularly if it's extended, is that it's probably someone close, a family member, a neighbor, someone like that."

"Yes," Weiss said.

"Have any sense if it was more than one person?"

"Probably one."

"Are you sure?" I said.

Again, Weiss looked thoughtful.

"About how many molested her? No."

"But that she was molested?"

"Yes," he said. "I cannot prove it. I cannot even demonstrate logically why I believe it. But yes, I am at some intuitive level sure."

I nodded.

"I got no problem with intuitive," I said. "Most of what I do is not the result of pure reason."

"That's true of most people," Weiss said. "Not all of them know it."

"Sure," I said. "Anything else you can tell me about Adelaide?"

"Not really. When her mother took her I urged that she see a competent therapist," Weiss said. "I told her I could help with a referral, and in any case was always available to her new therapist or to Adelaide. Mrs. Bradshaw declined a referral."

"Ever hear from anyone?"

"No."

"You think she got better?"

"Not without a good deal of professional attention," Weiss said.

ROUGH WEATHER

# 47

*When Hawk and I got to* my office we found a man and a woman waiting in the corridor. I unlocked the door and we went in. Hawk went and sat on Pearl's couch and put his feet on the coffee table. I went to my desk. The man and woman sat in front of my desk. I introduced myself.

"We're the Lessards," the man said.

They were both tall and athletic-looking. About fifty. Probably played a lot of tennis. Probably in a southern clime; they were both tanned. His hair was gray. Hers was blond and firmly in place.

"It was our son who was killed at Tashtego," the woman said.

"I'm very sorry for your loss," I said.

They nodded. They were both aware of Hawk behind them.

"May we speak freely?" Mrs. Lessard said.

"Absolutely. I share everything with my associate," I said.

They both turned to look at him. Hawk smiled reassuringly.

"You were there," Mr. Lessard said.

"Yes," I said. "I'm sorry I couldn't have prevented it."

"We know," Mrs. Lessard said. "The police have explained everything to us."

"It was the police who sent us to you," Lessard said. "A Captain Healy, who is apparently in charge of the investigation."

"Nobody better," I said.

"He told us you've been investigating," Mrs. Lessard said.

"I'm trying to find Adelaide," I said.

"Yes. We gave Heidi some money to meet the ransom demands, but so far Adelaide is still missing."

"Heidi didn't have the money?" I said.

"She said it would take her too long to convert it to cash, and was afraid to wait," Lessard said. "We gave her the money as an advance against Adelaide's substantial inheritance from . . ." He stopped, and took in some air before he seemed able to say the name. ". . . Maurice."

"Where did they meet?" I said.

"Maurice and Adelaide? They were friends in college."

"Which college?"

"Penn," Mr. Lessard said. "Maurice graduated two years ago. Adelaide was a freshman when my son was a junior. We hadn't really known much about her until he announced they were getting married."

"How'd you feel about that?" I said.

"We heard she came from a good family," Lessard said.

"We were thrilled," Mrs. Lessard said. "Poor Maurice had very few girlfriends. We always feared he might be gay."

**Feared**.

They were quiet then, very much with each other. Looking back in their memories at things they would never see again, feeling things they probably couldn't express.

"Will the ransom payment make a significant dent in the inheritance?" I said.

"Oh, no," Mr. Lessard said. "No, no. It is a substantial inheritance."

I nodded.

"And what can I do for you?" I said.

"We don't know," Mr. Lessard said. "Do you have any idea why this happened?"

"It's just so awful," Mrs. Lessard said. "We can't let go of it. We have to do something. We don't even know what."

"Maybe if somehow we could help you catch him," Lessard said.

"We have scads of money," Mrs. Lessard said. "We can pay you anything."

"No need," I said. "This happened right under my nose and I didn't prevent it. I have to even that up."

"Whether we pay you or not," Lessard said.

"Yes."

"You know who shot him."

"Of course," I said. "I saw him do it. The police must have told you about Rugar."

"Yes. But there's no sense to it," Lessard said.

"We have to make sense of it," Mrs. Lessard said.

"Do you have other children?" I said.

"We have a daughter, in her second year at Princeton."

"Perhaps I should talk with her," I said.

# 48

*It was late afternoon* and dark when Hawk and I finished running intervals at the Harvard track. We walked across the Anderson Bridge, waiting for our oxygen levels to renew themselves, and on up through Harvard Square and along Mass Ave to Linnaean Street. Susan was going to make dinner for us.

"She actually gonna make it herself," Hawk said, "or is she ordering it on the phone?"

"Says she's making it herself," I said.

"Ain't that kind of dangerous?" Hawk said.

"Yes," I said.

Susan was still with her last patient when we went into her house and up the stairs to Susan's apartment, where we had changed into our sweats earlier. Pearl was pleased to see us again, and ran around the apartment with a squeaky toy in her mouth, which made her sound like the Road Runner. *Beep, beep.*

"She do that every time she see you?" Hawk said.

"When you get out of the shower," I said, "she'll do it again."

"Nothing wrong with enthusiasm," Hawk said, and went in to take a shower.

While he showered, I fed Pearl, and when Hawk was finished and dressed, I went in and did the same thing. When I came out, Pearl ran around with her squeaky toy. *Beep, beep.*

"You right," Hawk said. "She done that with me, too."

Then, glowing with health, both of us breathing normally again, clean, sober, and looking good, we had a drink.

"Table been set already," Hawk said.

"She probably did it last night," I said.

"Plan ahead," Hawk said.

"Looks nice," I said. "Tablecloth, crystal, flowers in the middle. Linen napkins."

"I eat dinner at your house," Hawk said, "we stand at the counter and eat pizza from the box."

"I'm an informal guy," I said.

"She doing this 'cause I'm here?" Hawk said.

"Whenever we eat together," I said, "just she and I, she does this."

"She like to do things right," Hawk said.

"Yes."

"Me, too," Hawk said.

"Different things," I said.

"True," Hawk said, "but you gonna do it some way, might as well be right."

Susan came in through the front door. Pearl dashed around. *Beep, beep.* Susan kissed her, and Hawk, and me.

"I don't mind you kissing the dog before me," I said. "But Hawk?"

"He was closer," Susan said.

"And better," Hawk said.

"Want a drink?" I said.

"Will you make me a martini while I change?"

"Up with lots of olives," I said.

"Two minutes," she said, and went into the bedroom.

I got up and mixed the martini in the shaker and put the olives in her glass. I didn't add ice to the shaker.

"She like it warm?" Hawk said.

"No, but I don't want the ice to melt and ruin the martini."

"She say two minutes."

"She thinks it will be two minutes. When she comes out, she'll think it was two minutes."

"But it won't be," Hawk said.

"Be about twenty," I said.

In fact, it was twenty-five. When she emerged from the bedroom in jeans and a sleeveless top, I put ice in the shaker and finished the martini.

Susan took her drink to the couch and sat down beside Pearl and tucked her legs up under her. In the sleeveless top, her arms showed muscle definition.

"Met a guy in western Mass," I said, "named Weiss. Says you're very beautiful."

"Weiss," she said. "Is he a therapist?"

"Yeah, in Ashfield."

"Springfield, really," Susan said. "I remember him. He lives in Ashfield and sees patients in his home a couple of days a week."

"So you know him."

"I've met him. I never knew he thought I was beautiful," she said.

"He competent?"

"Who cares?" Susan said. "He thinks I'm beautiful."

"He tells me that Adelaide Van Meer was probably molested sexually as a child."

"Does she say so?"

"No," I said. "But she tried to commit suicide, and when he talked with her in the hospital he formed an intuitive opinion."

Susan nodded. Pearl shifted so that her head hung off the couch and her feet stuck up in the air resting against the back of the couch. Susan rubbed Pearl's stomach.

"I don't know him well," Susan said. "Met him at a couple of conferences. I have no reason to question his competence."

"What do you think about intuitive opinions," I said.

"Probably what you do," Susan said. "I

prefer tangible support, but sometimes if it is unavailable, intuition may have to do."

"And intuition ain't licking it off a stone," Hawk said. "It what you know. What you've seen and heard and smelled. People you've known who are like this person."

Susan smiled.

"Experience," Susan said.

"The very word," Hawk said.

"He thinks it's someone close to the family," I said.

"It usually is," Susan said.

"Talk to me about symptoms," I said.

"Of childhood sexual abuse?" Susan said. "Low self-esteem, dependency, pro-miscuity, and at the same time trouble with intimacy, a kind of frantic aimlessness, fear of the unknown. Some or any of these, or none, or other symptoms, depending on the person."

"Do people get over it?"

"You mean without help?" Susan said.

"Yeah."

"If they do," Susan said, "we never see them and thus don't know. I would guess that it would be unusual."

"Her mother came and took her home

as soon as she could leave the hospital. Weiss recommended therapy," I said. "Any way to know if she's seen a shrink around here?"

"Other than asking her, or her mother," Susan said, "none that I can think of."

"Family doctor, maybe," I said.

"If the shrink went to her," Hawk said, "be a security log on him."

I stared at him for a moment.

"The Tashtego patrol," I said.

"Uh-huh."

"Security log," I said. "And all this time I thought you were just another ugly face."

Hawk ignored me.

"What's for supper," he said to Susan.

"We begin with a wedge of iceberg lettuce with ranch dressing. Then a recipe I saw in the *Times*. Noodles with ground lamb, pistachio nuts, oregano, and a béchamel sauce."

Hawk said, "Wow!"

"It will be delicious," Susan said.

"You think?" Hawk said.

"I will stake my reputation on it," Susan said.

"As a cook?" Hawk said.

"Absolutely."

"Susan," Hawk said. "You ain't got no reputation as a cook."

"I will," she said, "after you wrap your chops around this meal."

"That good," I said.

"That good," Susan said. "Maybe better."

And incredibly, it was.

# 49

*Hawk and I were in Providence* in the offices of Absolute Security, talking to Artie Fonseca.

"Security logs?" Fonseca said.

"You saying you didn't keep any?"

"Well, sure," he said, "we kept them. But they are for our internal use only. I couldn't release them to you without explicit instructions from Mrs. Bradshaw."

"How many of your people got killed," I said, "when the wedding thing went down?"

"Four," Fonseca said. "You know that."

"And what did you say to me about that?"

"Sure, I know. I said anything I could do to help . . . but the cops already got the whole wedding list. What good will the daily logs do you, going back five years?"

"I want to see if there's a shrink that was treating Adelaide."

"The daughter? Why?"

"If there is one," I said, "I'd like to talk to him."

"Man," Fonseca said. "I can't . . ."

I looked at Hawk.

"Four of his people," I said to Hawk. "Killed without a chance. Didn't even get the holsters unsnapped."

"Man don't seem to care," Hawk said.

"There's a confidentiality clause in the contract," Fonseca said. "I violate it, we lose the account. I gotta think of the guys working for me now. They'd be out of work."

"No," I said. "You violate it, *and they find out*, you might lose the account."

"And you won't tell them."

"No."

"How about him?" Fonseca said, nodding at Hawk.

"Hawk? He doesn't tell anybody anything," I said. "Even when he should."

Hawk smiled happily.

"Jesus, Spenser," Fonseca said. "You
got me in a bind."

"Simple business," I said. "Either you let
somebody gun down four of your people
like vermin and walk away from it, or you
do what you can to even it up."

Fonseca stood and walked across the
room. He got a bottle of water out of a
small refrigerator.

"You guys want any water?" he said.

Hawk and I shook our heads. Fonseca
walked back to his desk and sat down. He
unscrewed the top on the bottle of water
and drank some.

"Gotta stay hydrated," he said.

I waited. Hawk waited. Fonseca looked
at the water bottle. Then he looked out his
window at the Providence River. Then he
looked back at me.

"Okay," he said, "we got the logs com-
puterized. You can read them off the screen.
You know how to use a computer?"

"Sort of," I said.

Fonseca sat down, clacked around with

his computer for a moment, and then nodded at the screen.

"You know how to scroll through?" he said.

"Yes," I said.

Fonseca stood and gestured to his chair.

"Be my guest," he said.

# 50

*Wearing jeans and a fluffy jacket,* Susan came into my office in the middle of the afternoon. With her came the barely discernible scent of her perfume, and the apparent force of her self.

"No patients?" I said.

"Teaching day," Susan said, "every Wednesday."

"Oh, yeah," I said. "Classes over?"

"They are."

"You want to sit on my lap?" I said.

"No," Susan said. "I looked into your Dr. Rosselli."

"And?"

Susan took off her fluffy jacket and settled in to one of my client chairs.

"He's not a psychiatrist," Susan said. "His training is in urology. But he does emotional counseling and therapy."

"Dr. Feelgood?" I said.

"That seems the consensus," Susan said. "Dispenses and administers psychopharmacologic products to an elite list of wealthy clients."

"And I'll bet he makes house calls," I said.

"He does."

"Is he doing anything illegal?" I said.

"Not on the surface. My colleagues are contemptuous of him, but any licensed physician can counsel and prescribe."

"But he can't call himself a psychiatrist?"

"Not without a psychiatric residency," Susan said.

"How about psychopharmacology," I said. "Is it effective?"

"Often," Susan said. "Depends on the patient and the disorder."

"But," I said.

"Not all disorders are manageable by drugs, and if they are used anyway, they can at the very least impede a cure by masking the symptoms."

"How about a kid who's been sexually molested?" I said.

"It is debatable," Susan said.

"Would you use drugs in such a case?"

"I'm a psychologist," Susan said. "Not a psychiatrist. So I can't prescribe. When it's indicated, I have a psychiatrist prescribe for me."

"Would it seem indicated in the case of Adelaide Van Meer?"

She shifted a little in the chair and crossed her legs. Her jeans fit her as if they'd been personally designed for her by Levi Strauss himself.

"I am not being cautious," she said. "It's you and me. But I honestly can't say. I've never talked with Adelaide Van Meer. I saw her briefly and unfortunately at the wedding. My only information is third-hand, originating with a shrink who is guessing."

I nodded.

"He could be helping, he could be hurting," I said.

"Yes," Susan said. "But all of us in the, ah, healing business run that risk."

"He seems. to have gone regularly to

the island," I said, "ever since her attempted suicide."

"He's obviously doing something out there," Susan said. "It would do you no harm to find out what."

"I will," I said. "Now do you want to sit on my lap."

Susan smiled.

"Maybe later," she said.

# 51

Emil Rosselli, M.D., had some very nice office space in a professional building on Route 9 in Chestnut Hill. There was a soft smell of flowers, the sound of quiet music. There was expensive carpeting, and a receptionist with excellent thighs. She and I were both pleased about her thighs, I think. And she allowed me to look at them for a while as I waited for the doctor.

After an appropriate wait, I was taken into the office. It was all white, with indirect lighting and a lot of plants. He was tall and handsome, and looked like the father many people might wish they had . . . wavy gray hair brushed straight back, even white teeth, calm eyes. Just the man to help you with your problem. His dark blue suit contrasted strikingly with his office.

He gestured me to a chair and sat back quietly with his hands folded on his desk. The desktop was clear except for a futuristic phone.

"I'm Dr. Rosselli," he said.

I put my card on the desk where he could see it.

"That would have been my guess," I said. "My name is Spenser. I'm a detective."

He nodded gravely.

"You're treating Adelaide Van Meer," I said.

Rosselli didn't say anything. He simply raised his eyebrows.

"You go regularly every two weeks to Tashtego Island and have done so since shortly after she attempted suicide five years ago."

Rosselli pursed his lips.

"I'm curious about her condition," I said.

He put them both together, pursing his lips and arching his eyebrows. Artful. I waited. He waited. I had a lot of experience at waiting. Apparently, so did he. It was turning into a wait-off when he probably figured that time is money and decided to cut it off.

"I am a physician," he said. "If I were treating this person and she did have a condition, patient confidentiality would prevent me from speaking of it."

I waited a little more, just to prove that I could, and then I said, "Not only are these questions of interest to me, they are of pressing interest to the Boston Police, the Massachusetts State Police, and the Federal Bureau of Investigation."

Rosselli smiled faintly.

"You can discuss it quietly with me," I said, "and suffer no ill effects, or I can get representatives from all three of the aforementioned agencies in here to tear your life apart."

He stared at me for a moment. Then he said, "Perhaps I should call my attorney."

I raised my eyebrows and said nothing. He leaned forward and put his hand on the phone. I pursed my lips. After a time he leaned back from the phone.

"What specifically would you like to know?" he said.

"What are you treating her for?"

"Neurasthenia," he said.

"Do people still suffer from that?" I said.

He made a slight dismissive motion of his head. Next question.

"How are you treating her?"

"Counseling and medication," he said.

"What are the medications?"

"Nothing you would be likely to understand," Rosselli said.

"Doubtless you're right," I said. "Give me a list."

"Why?"

"So I may show it to someone who will understand it."

Rosselli shook his head.

"I'm sorry, that is really just too intrusive."

"Which cops would you like to give it to?" I said. "City, state, or federal?"

He sat in silence for another time. I thought about arching my brows *and* pursing my lips, but decided it was overacting. Then he leaned to his phone and pressed a button.

"Betsy," he said. "Please bring me the protocol for Adelaide Van Meer."

We waited, and in a minute or so, Ms. Thighs glided in with a printout page and handed it to Rosselli. He shook his head and nodded at me. She widened her eyes and gave me the printout. It seemed to be legit. I folded it and put it in my inside pocket. Ms. Thighs glided out.

"Would, ah, neurasthenia be causative in her suicide attempt?" I said.

"She denies that there ever was a suicide attempt," Rosselli said. "But certainly neurasthenia can lead one to attempt it."

"Was she ever sexually molested?" I said.

Rosselli seemed almost to recoil, as if I had suddenly shown him something repulsive.

"Molested?" he said.

I nodded enthusiastically.

"Of course not," he said.

"How can you be so sure?" I said.

"I would certainly have learned of it in the five years I've been treating her," he said.

I nodded.

"Do you know what causes her to be neurasthenic?" I said.

"Exhaustion of the nervous system," he said. "It's probably more characterological than anything else."

"And it manifests itself how?" I said.

"Fatigue, depression, general discomfort with no objective cause or lesions."

I said, "Thank you, Dr. Rosselli," and stood up.

He stood and walked me to the door.

"I trust there will be no need for the police," he said.

"No, of course not, no need at all," I said.

He opened the door for me, and I walked out, past Ms. Thighs.

# 52

*I had worked a few years* back on a school shooting in Dowling, out in the middle of the state. During the time Susan was away, and I needed a shrink to talk with my client, and she had suggested a guy named Dix who used to be a cop. It had worked out well, which was why Susan and I went to see him about Dr. Rosselli.

He had a clean-shaven head and big square hands, and he looked as if he could still put a stranglehold on someone if he had to. He stood when we came into his office.

"Susan," he said. "Nice to see you again."

He looked at me.

"Whaddya got?"

I handed him the list of meds that I'd gotten from Rosselli. He looked at it without comment.

Susan said, "I've gone through this stuff, and I have an opinion, but I'm not sufficiently expert in psychopharmacology."

"What are they being used for?" Dix said.

Susan smiled.

"To treat neurasthenia," she said.

"Neurasthenia?" Dix said.

"That's what the man told me," I said.

"For crissake," Dix said. "That's like saying it's being used to treat the vapors."

"I've explained that to him," Susan said.

"Who is this doctor," Dix said. "Is he a shrink?"

"His M.D. is urology," Susan said. "He bills himself as a therapeutic counselor."

"Rosselli," Dix said.

"You know him?" I said.

"Emil Rosselli," Dix said. "That's who it is, isn't it?"

"Yes," I said. "What do you think of him?"

"Dope dealer to the rich and famous," Dix said. "He's a fucking disgrace."

"Don't get too technical on me," I said.

"I simply strive for accuracy," Dix said.

He scanned the list.

"There's some vitamins here," he said, "which probably do no harm, and the rest are psychotropic drugs."

"Like sedatives?" I said.

"Some," he said. "There's an assortment to get you up, calm you down, get a balance between. All of them have legitimate uses, but they are not normally used in this amount or these combinations."

"Pills?" I said.

"Some pills, some injectables, some that come in either form," Dix said. "I can't tell from the list how often the patient received this stuff."

"He went there every two weeks," I said.

"Doesn't tell me if he gave her the same thing every time," Dix said.

"The more he went, I suppose, the more money he made."

"Most Feelgoods use injections," Dix said. "Patient can take pills himself, but the doc can jack up the price if the patient thinks he always has to get a shot."

"Maybe he also did counseling," I said.

"I hope not," Dix said.

"What would be the effect of these drugs on the recipient?" I said.

"It can vary," Dix said. "But certainly it would dull her response to the phenomenological world."

"How about on a young woman who had been sexually molested and attempted suicide."

"Palliative at best," Dix said.

"Harmful?" I said.

"The actual drugs? Can't say without more information. But if she is suffering severe post-molestation psychopathology, it's like putting a Band-Aid over gangrene."

"The pathology will continue to fester," I said.

"A bit dramatic maybe," Dix said, "but yes. She will continue to need help."

"But not from Emil Rosselli," I said.

"First do no harm," Dix said.

"I think Rosselli is governed by a different code," I said.

Dix smiled.

"Show me the money," he said.

# 53

*In the late afternoon,* Hawk and I sat with Valerie Lessard in a big wooden booth in the taproom at the Nassau Inn in Princeton. The room looked like it was supposed to, with dark wood and murals. Valerie had some white wine; Hawk and I drank beer.

"The thing about poor Maurice," Valerie said, "is he was gay."

"Was he out?" I said.

"Not around my parents," Valerie said.

"They didn't know?"

Valerie, as she talked, was obliquely studying Hawk.

"He didn't want them to," Valerie said.

"Would they disapprove?" I said.

"I don't think so," Valerie said. "Plus, hell, they knew. Anyone who spent time with my brother would know."

"They talk with you about it?"

Still appraising Hawk, Valerie nodded her head.

"Sure," she said. "Not, did I think he was gay? More, did I know his friends? Did he have any girlfriends? Was he happy?"

"You and your brother get along?"

"Yeah," Valerie said. "I liked him. He was really sweet. We could talk. More like having a sister than a brother, I guess. Except we didn't have to compete for dates."

"Did he date?"

"No."

"Men or women?"

"No. I don't know for sure if he ever had sex with anyone," she said.

"Did he tell you he was gay?"

"Not in so many words," Valerie said. "But we both knew that we both knew, if you know what I'm saying."

"I do," I said. "How did he end up with Adelaide Van Meer?"

"School. He was a junior when she was a freshman. They got to be friends. Not boyfriend, girlfriend. Just friends. Except for me, she might have been his first close friend. Two lost souls, I guess . . ."

Valerie stopped for a moment and looked at the tabletop. Her eyes were teary, but she didn't cry.

"Poor Maurice," she said finally.

"Adelaide was lost, too?" I said.

"Yeah. She was sort of withdrawn and, like, fearful, and mad, all at the same time. Conflicted, maybe," Valerie said. "I'm not sure if she was straight." Valerie smiled and sort of shrugged. "I'm a psych major."

"No shame in it," I said.

She nodded and finished her wine and looked toward the bar.

Hawk stood and said, "Chardonnay?"

She smiled at him and nodded. He went to the bar.

"So how did it develop from friendship to marriage?" I said.

She shrugged.

"I guess they started going to, you know, parties together, and people started to treat them like a couple. And one day he brought her home for the weekend. I don't remember the occasion. Maybe one of those big rowing events on the Schuylkill."

Hawk returned with her wine. She smiled very brightly at him. She was a nice-looking kid in the way that rich kids can be. Nice teeth, nice skin, good body, good haircut. I was never clear how I could tell, but money always seemed to show. She drank some wine.

"Anyway, my mother and father, well, I guess, more my mother, went crazy," Valerie said. "Maurice had a girlfriend! You know?"

"Did she push him into it?"

"My mom can be a little pushy, but I don't know. I went away to school, and whatever developed developed without me."

"He didn't talk about it?" I said.

"To me? Not really. He said he felt bad for Adelaide. That she'd had a pretty bad childhood, but he never said exactly what."

"You think he married her to help her out?" I said.

"I don't know. I mean, I wasn't around. I was pretty busy here. Classes and dating and all," Valerie said. "Hell, he was queer, she might have been a lesbian, maybe they thought they could be each other's beard. You know?"

I nodded. Hawk and I had finished our beer. Valerie was almost through her second wine. She looked at Hawk.

"Are you a detective, too?" she said.

Hawk smiled at her.

"No, ma'am, ah jess come along to carry his luggage," Hawk said.

"He doesn't seem to have any luggage," Valerie said.

"Easy job," Hawk said.

Valerie smiled again, staring at him directly now.

"You spending the night in town?" she said.

"Uh-uh," Hawk said.

"Want to buy me dinner?" Valerie said.

"How old are you?" Hawk said.

"I'll be twenty in the spring," she said.

"And I won't," Hawk said.

"So what?" Valerie said.

Hawk smiled at her again and shook his head.

"You good-looking and you nice," Hawk said. "But you too young."

"You'd be surprised," Valerie said.

"No doubt that I would," Hawk said. "And I thank you for the offer. But I be having dinner with my age mate here. He's boring, but he's boring about things I know."

She shrugged.

"No harm trying," Valerie said.

"None," Hawk said.

"Boring?" I said to Hawk.

# 54

*I was back in Boston,* in my office, discussing with Hawk the official weekday start of the cocktail hour.

"You don't have to wait for no damn time," Hawk said. "You want a drink, have a drink."

"At ten in the morning?" I said.

"That when you want it, yes."

"How uncivilized," I said.

"I is of African heritage," Hawk said. "'Course I uncivilized."

"True, while I am a descendant of Irish kings."

"Which be why you wanting a drink at ten in the morning," Hawk said.

"Not always," I said.

"So what we talking about?" Hawk said.

"It's four-thirty," I said. "Half-hour to go." Hawk shook his head.

"Weird," Hawk said.

"How about yesterday?" I said. "You wouldn't respond to a good-looking college girl who came on to you."

"Too young," Hawk said.

"She's a full-grown woman, almost twenty, anatomically correct. What's too young."

"She talked funny," Hawk said. "You know, like they all do. High voice, nasal, talk very fast. Grating."

"Well, yeah. But how much talking were you expecting?"

"She say dinner," Hawk said. "That be chitchat. She say want me to come to your room now? Be different."

"Man," I said. "I didn't know you had limits."

"Like to have sex with women who was at least born when John Carlos and Tommie Smith was in Mexico," Hawk said.

"Wow," I said. "And here I am thinking you required only a pulse."

Hawk grinned.

"Also depends what else I got on my plate at the time," he said.

"Glad it's going well for you," I said.

"Yowzah," Hawk said, with the accent on the *zah*.

My phone rang. It was Bradshaw.

"I gotta see you," he said. "Now."

"Where are you?" I said.

"Wagner Motel on One twenty-eight in Burlington," he said. "Across from the mall."

"What do you need?"

"I need help," he said. "I'm in danger. You need to come right now."

"Okay," I said.

"I'm in room two-oh-three, under the name Bailey."

"Here we come," I said.

"We?"

"My associate Hawk will be with me. Big man, black, don't panic if you see him."

"Nobody else," he said. "No one knows I'm here."

"Mum's the word," I said.

"Hurry up," he said. "Just get here quick."

I hung up. And looked at Hawk.

"Gotta go rescue Bradshaw," I said.

"From what?"

"Don't know," I said. "He said to hurry."

"There go the cocktail hour," Hawk said.

"We can stop in a packy," I said. "Maybe buy a couple of nips for the car."

"Pathetic," Hawk said.

"I know," I said. "I thought so when I said it."

# 55

*The Wagner Motel* was an undistinguished suburban motel on a major highway near a big shopping center. It had a central building where the front desk, bar, and restaurant were. There was a wing on each side. Hawk and I went in the side door of one of the wings and up the stairs without passing the front desk. We were at room 323. Room 203 was at the other end. When we got there the privacy sign was hanging on the doorknob. Hawk stepped to the side. I knocked on the door. Nobody answered. I knocked a couple more times. It seemed pretty clear that there were no plans to open the door.

I put my ear to the door. The television was playing loudly. I looked at Hawk. He shrugged.

"Call the manager or kick it in?" he said.

"Call," I said.

We were at the end of the corridor. I went to the house phone on the small lamp table. In a minute or two a nervous-looking young guy with an ineffective combover got out of the elevator and walked down the hall to us. He looked uneasily at Hawk. Then at me.

"You the man that called?" he said.

"Yes," I said.

"Are you guests of the hotel?" he said.

"No. We were invited here by the occupant of this room," I said. "We fear something untoward might have happened."

The desk guy was wearing a white shirt with a green tie and a green vest. The collar on the shirt was curled up at the tips.

"Untoward?" he said.

I had a sense he might not be on the fast track.

"I'm a detective," I said. "Working on a case. We need the door opened."

"I can't just override his privacy sign," the desk guy said.

From outside the motel there was the dim sound of a siren being turned off.

"Ah," I said.

"I took the liberty of calling the police," the desk guy said. "I will wait for them, if you don't mind."

In maybe a minute, two Burlington cops came out of the elevator and walked down to us. Both were young guys who looked at if they got a lot of exercise. They were carrying their nightsticks.

"What's the deal," one of them said.

"My name is Spenser," I said. "I'm working with a state police captain named Healy on a case."

"I know Healy. What's the case?"

"Has to do with the kidnapping a while ago on Tashtego Island."

"Yeah," the cop said. "I remember that. No progress is what I heard."

"We might make some," I said, "if we can get this door unlocked."

The cop looked at Hawk.

"Who's this," he said.

"My partner," I said.

Hawk had no expression.

"Tell me more," the cop said.

His partner had taken a few steps away and stood quietly watching Hawk and me. Especially Hawk.

"Guy called me and said he was in trouble and needed to see me right away."

"Guy in this room?"

"Yeah. He's registered as Bailey, but his real name is Bradshaw."

"Like the Bradshaw broad on Tashtego?"

"Estranged husband," I said.

The cop nodded at the desk guy.

"Open the door," he said.

The desk guy did. The door opened a couple of inches and held.

"Security chain," the desk guy said.

"Mr. Bradshaw?" the cop said. "It's the police, Mr. Bradshaw."

Nothing.

"Kick it in," the cop said.

"Me?" the desk guy said.

Hawk grinned.

"Me," he said.

He shifted his weight and drove his right foot into the door just above the knob. The safety chain tore out of the doorjamb and the door banged open. The cop went past Hawk into the room and stopped. I went in behind him. The window opposite the door had a bullet hole in it with spiderweb fracture lines spreading across the pane. On the floor, on his back, in front of the window, with a bullet hole in his forehead and a spread of blood soaking into the rug beneath, was the late Harden Bradshaw. The cop bent over and felt for a pulse.

"Gone," he said after a moment.

"Blood's starting to dry," I said.

The cop nodded and yelled to his partner in the hall.

"Call the captain, Harry," he said. "We got a homicide."

Then he looked at me.

"You and your partner stick around," he said.

# 56

*When all the crime-scene fuss* was over, the place dusted, the photographs taken, the grounds searched, the room sealed, Healy sat with Hawk and me in the coffee shop of the motel and ate a sandwich.

Healy put his sandwich down and swallowed and looked at Hawk.

"I seem to be consorting with a known felon," Healy said.

"Think how I feel," Hawk said.

Healy nodded.

"Motel's dug into a sort of low hillside," Healy said. "So ten feet from the back, there's a hill nearly level with the second floor."

"Shoulda asked for a front room," Hawk said.

Healy nodded and ate some of his sandwich. Hawk and I each had a beer. We were hoping to do better than the Wagner Coffee Shop for dinner.

"Footprints on the hill?" I said.

"Nope, ground's dry. Lotta people have walked around up there; grass is sort of trampled."

"Peeping Toms?" I said.

"Everybody needs a nice hobby," Healy said.

"So whoever shot him knew where he was and was good with a gun. Put one in Bradshaw's head through the glass," I said.

"From maybe twenty feet," Healy said. "Didn't have to be Annie Oakley."

"One shot," I said. "That's confidence."

"Maybe, but from the hill you can't see the floor of the room," Healy said. "When Bradshaw went down, he was out of sight."

"One in the middle of the forehead, one try only?" I said. "Guy must have had some confidence in himself, unless he was aiming for the middle of the mass and missed badly."

"Wasn't Bradshaw some sort of spook?" Hawk said.

"Maybe," I said.

"He knew he in danger," Hawk said. "Why he called you."

"That's what he said."

"Shoulda known better than hide in a room at somebody's eye level," Hawk said.

"And stand looking out the window with the lights on," Healy said. "There was a scatter of glass particles on his face."

"Maybe he wasn't a spook," I said.

"Maybe not too bright," Hawk said.

"Fear makes you stupid sometimes," I said.

Hawk grinned.

"Wouldn't know," he said.

"He thought no one knew he was in the motel," I said.

Hawk nodded.

"Hole looks like a small-caliber, and we found a twenty-two slug in the mattress," Healy said. "Maybe a target gun."

"Which means the shooter's a pro," I said. "Or such an amateur that it was the only gun he could get."

"I'm voting for pro," Healy said.

"So who we got in this mess that's a pro?" I said.

"Tony Marcus," Healy said. "Actually, Ty-Bop."

"Ty-Bop's just the gun," I said. "Tony pulls the trigger."

"I know," Healy said.

"Or Rugar," Hawk said.

"I think that's a union violation," I said. "You're detecting."

"Nope," Hawk said. "Just thinking out loud. Prove that I can."

"Why would Rugar kill this guy?" Healy said.

"We knew that," I said, "we might know everything."

"Wouldn't that be refreshing," Healy said.

# 57

*It was Sunday.* We were at the counter of the Agawam Diner, the world's leading restaurant, having a late breakfast. Hawk had taken Sunday off, on the hopeful assumption that no one in Rowley would try to kill me. From where we sat I could see that Pearl had settled down in the driver's seat of my car and gone to sleep just as if she didn't know we were in there eating without her.

"I got a call," I said, "from Heidi Bradshaw."

"Really."

"She wants to see me."

"Of course she does," Susan said. "Who wouldn't."

"She sounded sort of scared," I said.

"Of what?"

"She'd heard about Bradshaw," I said. "I think she's scared it will happen to her."

"She say why she thinks that?"

"No."

"Be good to know," Susan said.

"It would," I said. "Any other questions you think I should ask?"

"None, I'm sure, that you haven't thought of," Susan said. "Myself, I would be very interested in why she didn't get better psychiatric treatment for her daughter after she attempted suicide."

"Yeah," I said. "I'd like to know that, too. I would also like to know if she knew Rugar in Bucharest."

"Do you think she'll tell you?"

"Probably not," I said. "But something might come out."

"Nothing ventured . . ." Susan said. "Are you going there?"

"No," I said. "She's coming to me."

"Noblesse oblige," Susan said.

"Yes," I said. "I'm thrilled."

"Have you ever thought about how much

it must cost," Susan said, "to be Heidi Bradshaw?"

"More than the GNP of Albania?" I said.

"Probably," Susan said. "She doesn't spin, neither does she sow."

"She's dependent on the kindness of husbands," I said.

Susan nodded.

"The most recent of whom seem to be broke, or nearly so," I said. "According to Epstein."

"Might want to factor that in," Susan said.

"Yeah," I said. "You know what I don't get? Epstein says Van Meer is broke. Van Meer says he's rich."

"Drunks are the royalty of denial," Susan said.

"Especially while drinking," I said.

"Which for someone like Van Meer is probably nearly always," Susan said.

"Maybe that's why he drinks. Denial is a much more pleasant reality than the one he'd have to face," I said.

"Maybe," Susan said. "Some people drink because they like it, you know, and then get addicted and drink because they must."

"I'm still at the *like it* part," I said.

"You won't get addicted," Susan said.

We were both drinking coffee. Susan had ordered a soft-boiled egg and some toast. I went a bit heartier: orange juice, three eggs over easy, sausages, home fries, toast, and of course, the basis of all gourmet breakfasts, pie.

"Why not?"

"You won't," she said.

"I'm kind of addicted to you," I said.

"That's because you love me," Susan said.

"And I don't love booze?"

"No," Susan said. "You don't, nor would you." She smiled. "You're much too loyal."

The waitress brought my orange juice. I drank some. She refilled both our coffee cups.

"Doesn't addiction mean that you are beyond controlling it?" I said.

"Which is why you would never have one," Susan said.

"Because I'm addicted to self-control?"

"Or not being controlled," Susan said. "You are much too autonomous to ever let something get hold of you . . . or someone."

"Except?" I said.

Susan smiled.

"Nope, not even me," she said. "There are, after all, things you will not do, even for me."

The waitress returned and put the soft-boiled egg in front of Susan and my breakfast in front of me.

"How'd you know which of us got the big plate?" I said.

The waitress stared at me for a moment. Then she looked at Susan and looked at me.

"Just a wild guess," she said. "You need anything else right now?"

We didn't.

"There's not much that I can think of that I wouldn't do," I said, "if you asked."

"It's because I know better than to ask," Susan said.

"That's crazy," I said.

"You'd do anything I asked?" Susan said.

"Absolutely," I said.

"Can I have your pie?" Susan said.

"No," I said. "Of course not."

# 58

*It was like a presidential visit.* First into my office were two Tashtego security guys in plain clothes with walkie-talkies.

"You Spenser?" one of them said.

"Yes, I am," I said.

They both looked at Hawk, who was sitting on Pearl's couch.

"Who's he?"

"Security consultant," I said. "His name's Hawk."

"He's with you?" the Tashtego patrol guy said.

"He is," I said. "No one else would have him."

Hawk smiled a friendly smile.

"Okay," the guy said. "We're bringing Mrs. Bradshaw in."

He spoke briefly into his walkie-talkie. Then he and his partner moved to stand on either side of the door. We waited. In a minute, four more security guys came to the door and stood aside and from among them, like an old Esther Williams water ballet, Heidi emerged and came into the office. She was wearing a fur coat, which she slid out of as she sat and let it drape over the back of her chair. She had on a stretchy, tight-fitting sleeveless black top and a camel-colored skirt. The skirt was short above black boots.

She looked around my office, her glance lingering on Hawk. Then she said, "Okay, Michael, you and the others can wait outside."

"Yes, ma'am," the security guy said. "Do you want the door left open?"

"No," she said. "Close it."

The men withdrew. The door closed, and there we were.

"Who is this gentleman?" Heidi said.

"My associate Hawk," I said.

"Oh, my," Heidi said.

Hawk nodded at her.

"He's as male as you are," Heidi said.

"But less winsome," I said.

"Whatever that means," Heidi said. "The two of you look like a testosterone commercial."

It was the funny, warm, sexy Heidi today. Full of flirtatious innuendo. She really wanted something.

"And it's all at your service," I said. "Whaddya need?"

Heidi was quiet for a moment. She looked at Hawk for a long time, and then at me. She crossed her legs.

"May I speak freely?" she said.

"Yes," I said.

She stretched a little in her chair so that her breasts pushed out. Then she put her head down and rubbed the bridge of her nose at the corners of her eyes.

"It's terrible what happened to poor Harden," she said softly. "Do you know who killed him?"

"Not yet," I said.

"Can you tell me anything?"

"He was hiding out in a motel in Burlington, Mass," I said. "Under the name Bailey. Somebody shot him in the head through the window of his hotel room."

"Why was he hiding out?" she said.

"Don't know."

Heidi turned to Hawk, and as she leaned a little forward in the chair, her skirt got shorter.

"Were you there?" she said.

"Yes, ma'am," Hawk said.

"Do you know anything?" she said.

"Same as Spenser," Hawk said.

She looked back at me.

"Do the police have a theory?" she said.

"Not yet," I said.

"You found him there."

"Yes."

"How did you happen to go there?"

"He called me," I said. "Told me he was in danger. Asked for help."

"And you were too late," she said.

"Yes."

"Why you?" she said.

"Good question," I said. "I haven't solved a crime in quite a long time."

She shook her head slowly.

"You inspire confidence," she said. "Something about you is reassuring."

I looked at Hawk. He had no expression on his face.

"And you need reassurance," I said.

"If it could happen to Harden . . ." she said.

"Hence the heavy security," I said.

"Exactly."

"And you want what from me?" I said.

"I want you to be my personal body-guard."

"In addition to the Tashtego patrol?" I said.

"They didn't protect my Adelaide," she said.

"Neither did I," I said.

"You weren't hired to," Heidi said.

She shifted again in her chair, leaning toward me. The skirt seemed to have edged farther up her thighs. Probably just an accident.

"Why was I hired?" I said.

She sat back quite suddenly and stared at me.

"I . . . . I told you already," she said, "when

I hired you. I'm not proud of it, I guess, but I needed a man to lean on."

"Like a fish needs a bicycle," I said.

She opened her mouth and her eyes widened. She closed her mouth. She narrowed her eyes. The gamut of emotion.

"What are you saying," she said after a while.

Her voice was breathy.

"I'm saying you don't lean on men. You use them. I'm saying that you were involved with something or someone that scared you," I told her. "And you wanted a tough guy around to help you if it went bad. I was the tough guy of choice."

"I don't . . . you think I knew what was going to happen? What an awful thing to think. My daughter is gone. My son-in-law is dead. I am the victim here. How dare you accuse me."

"Did you know your son-in-law was gay?" I said.

"That's a disgusting thing to say. Of course he wasn't gay. If he were gay, why would he be marrying my daughter?"

"My question exactly," I said.

"I came here asking for your help, and you say these things to me?"

"Did you know Rugar," I said to Heidi, "in Bucharest, in 1984?"

"What?"

"You were in Bucharest in 1984," I said. "With Bradshaw, who was working out of the American embassy. So was Rugar."

"That's absurd," Heidi said.

She was sitting stiffly upright in her chair now. Her knees were pressed together; the ascent of her skirt had halted at mid-thigh. Her elbows were on the arms of the chair. Her hands were clasped in front of her. She seemed to be breathing rapidly, as if she had sprinted a distance.

"Coulda happened," Hawk said helpfully.

"It didn't," Heidi said.

She was almost prim.

"Kind of a big coincidence, though," I said. "You're all in Bucharest at the same time, and then, twenty-two years later, he shows up at your daughter's wedding and kidnaps her."

"I don't care," Heidi said. "I never met him."

"Your daughter tried to commit suicide," I said, "five years ago. Tell me about that."

"You . . . you pig of a man," she said.

"How come the only help you got her is this quack Rosselli?"

She sat even straighter and seemed to gather in on herself. Her primness changed to sternness.

"My daughter did not attempt suicide," she said. "It was merely an accidental overdose of her medication."

"How do you accidentally take twenty pills?" I said.

"She did not take twenty pills," Heidi said. "She's a nervous girl, she needs help sleeping. Perhaps under the influence of her pills she forgot she had taken them and took some more."

"What's Dr. Rosselli treating her for?" I said.

"He's her doctor," Heidi said. "He's treating her general health."

"Shrink out in the Berkshires says he believes she was sexually molested," I said.

"By whom?" Heidi said.

"He doesn't know."

"Of course he doesn't know," she said.

"He says it's usually someone in or near the family."

"He's a back-country witch doctor, for God's sake," Heidi said. "Why on earth would anyone listen to him?"

"Did you know that Van Meer is broke," I said. "And Bradshaw was nearly so?"

"What has that got to do with my Adelaide?"

"Weren't they the primary source of income for you and Adelaide?" I said.

"Absolutely not. I am entirely independent."

"Since the moment Adelaide married Maurice Lessard?" I said.

"Goddamn you," Heidi said. "I will not be treated like this. I don't want you for a bodyguard or anything else."

She turned and walked out of my office. The security detail closed ranks around her.

She paused for a moment and looked back at me.

"Fuck you," she said.

And away they all went without closing

the door. Hawk looked at me with no expression.

"At least her position clear," he said.

"Does this mean I'm losing my charm?" I said.

"Yeah," Hawk said.

# 59

"*So, did she tell you anything?*" Susan said.

"She tell him 'Fuck you,'" Hawk said.

"Her, too," Susan said.

"I took it as a proposition," I said.

Susan smiled.

"The glass is always half full for you," she said.

We were having dinner at Davio's. Susan was doing something with a salad. Hawk appeared thrilled with his veal chop. I was having pasta with Bolognese sauce, which is what I always had. Traditions matter.

"Aside from 'Fuck you,'" Susan said, "did you learn anything else?"

"I confirmed my suspicion that she knows a lot and lies about it," I said.

"What do you think she knows?" Susan said.

"I think she knows pretty much everything," I said. "She knew about her daughter's suicide attempt, though she denied that it was a suicide attempt. I think she knew about her daughter's molestation. I think she knew Rugar from way back. I think she knows that her second and third husbands would no longer be able to support her. I think she cannot support herself. Her daughter's marriage to Lessard was probably providential."

"Even if he's dead?"

"Epstein says Adelaide inherits everything he would have, plus her husband's share of the business, according to the pre-nup."

"If Adelaide is alive," Susan said.

"Even if she's dead, her mother might be her heir," I said.

"My God," Susan said. "She wouldn't have her own daughter killed."

"She might," I said.

Susan nodded.

"If one of us can even think of it," she said, "someone could do it."

"Also the bridegroom, Maurice Lessard, was, according to his sister, gay."

"And he married Adelaide because?"

"She was his beard? She was gay, too, and they bearded each other?"

"The molestation might have a place in all of this," Susan said.

"Might," I said.

"She admit any of this?" Susan said.

"No."

"Hawk?" Susan said. "You were there."

"Spenser's right," Hawk said. "You sit and listen to her and you know she's scrambling for cover. You know she's lying."

Susan nodded and ate a little salad and sipped a little wine.

"Not for nothing," she said to Hawk, "but are you aware that, in those rare moments when you are perfectly serious, you lose your accent."

"I am," Hawk said.

Susan smiled.

"So if she knows all this stuff, and won't tell you, then doesn't that mean she's complicit?"

"Be my guess," I said.

"But exactly what is she complicit in?" Susan said.

"I don't know for sure," I said. "And it's all guesswork and intuition. The courts do not welcome intuition."

"But . . ." Susan said.

"But there's an awful lot of money in the mix."

"Cherchez la bread," Hawk said.

"Wow," I said. "Multicultural, too."

"But," Susan said. "Why all this huge huzzarah on the island? Kidnapping, shootings, and all that?"

"I been thinking about that, too," I said. "When I'm not admiring Hawk's linguistic range. I tried it from the other end, so to speak. If the deal on the island is so not Rugar, then who is it? If one were to throw a kidnapping, who would throw one like that?"

"Heidi," Susan said.

I looked at Hawk.

"See," I said. "Not just another pretty face."

"No," Hawk said. "Got nice legs, too."

"It is just the kind of overproduced extravaganza that people like Heidi would throw," Susan said. "Maybe she didn't expect all the killing. Certainly she couldn't have planned the hurricane. But . . ."

"Like a kidnapping thrown by a party planner," Hawk said.

"Yes," Susan said.

"But why would Rugar go along with it?" I said.

"Money?" Susan said.

"Always a good guess," I said. "But it is so against his nature."

Hawk nodded.

"Had to be something in addition to money," Hawk said.

"And what would be in addition to money?" Susan said.

"And you a shrink," Hawk said.

"Love," I said.

Hawk nodded. Susan nodded, too. We were silent.

"Rugar and Heidi?" Susan said after a while.

I turned my palms up. Hawk said nothing.

"Nothing is proven," Susan said.

"But some of it can be," I said. "Sooner or later we'll find out if Heidi knew Rugar. Sooner or later we'll get a look at her finances. Sooner or later we should be able to find out if Adelaide was abused and by whom."

"If she's alive," Hawk said.

I nodded.

"If she's alive," I said.

"You think she is?" Susan said.

"I don't know that she isn't," I said.

Susan nodded. She cut up a leaf of romaine lettuce and ate part of it, and drank some wine.

"Do you think Rugar killed Bradshaw?"

"Who in this mess more likely?" I said.

"Tony Marcus?"

"Nope, I believe him. I think he had Ty-Bop ace Leonard to sever himself from the whole business, and to remind his employees of the zero-tolerance rule."

"Why would Rugar kill Bradshaw?"

"Don't know. But if there's a connection back to Bucharest, we might be able to find out," I said.

"If Heidi is in collusion with Rugar," Susan said, "and if she tells him the truth, Rugar is smart enough to know that you have a handle on this whole thing, and that eventually you may be able to unravel it."

"Yes," I said.

"And he must know you well enough to know that you will stay with it, however long it takes."

"Yes."

"Which means he may decide it is time to take decisive action."

"Yes," I said.

"Why am I hanging around?" Hawk said.

"The two of you are formidable," Susan said.

Hawk and I both nodded.

"But so is Rugar," she said to me. "He almost killed you once."

"I wasn't around when that happened."

"True."

"I am around now," Hawk said.

"Yes," Susan said.

"Him against both of us?" Hawk said. "I like our chances."

Susan nodded slowly. She looked at me. I smiled and nodded. She looked back at Hawk.

"And you'll continue to hang around," she said.

"I will," he said.

"Until it's over," she said.

"Until there's no need for my skill set," Hawk said.

The waiter brought Susan a second glass of wine. For Susan, that was a binge. She sipped some of it and put the glass down.

"Hawk," she said, "in regard to me having nice legs?"

"Yes, ma'am."

"Thanks for noticing."

Hawk grinned at her.

"My pleasure," he said.

# 60

*I was reading* the morning *Globe* in my office with my feet on the desk. I had made coffee and was drinking some. It was a bright day outside, temperature in the forties, and the sun reflecting off the windows of the office tower across the street made my office bright. I read methodically. The newspaper had years ago become a ritual, and I did it every morning, starting at page one, and wading on to the end. Every year there were more stories about shoes, and celebrities, and hot restaurants, so that every year I read less. But I still checked every headline. I still read *Doonesbury* carefully, and *Tank McNamara*, and *Arlo & Janis*. I still took some time on the sports page, though even there, ever more space was devoted to the financial aspects of the games, which interested me less than the Bank of America annual report.

I was studying a strip called *Stone Soup*, which seemed pretty good, and might fill the void left by *Calvin & Hobbes*, when Maggie Lane came in to see me. She was wearing jeans, and boots, and a short leather jacket. Her hair was loose and looked sort of soft. She was wearing more makeup than I remembered, and looked somewhat less crisp and businesslike than she had on Tashtego Island. I did not feel passion welling, but she no longer made me think of Dick Butkus.

I offered her a seat. She took it. I gave her coffee. She took that. I went back behind my desk and sat down and tilted my chair back a little.

"What's up?" I said.

"I am no longer employed," she said, "by the Bradshaws."

"Bradshaws?" I said.

"Excuse me?"

"Plural?" I said. "Bradshaws?"

"Yes," she said. "It's what I wanted to speak to you about."

"Okay," I said.

"When I heard about poor Mr. Bradshaw being killed," Maggie Lane said, "I . . . The place is like a fortress now. Heidi is terrified. She won't leave the island except with a bunch of guards."

"I know," I said. "What's she terrified of?"

"I assume whoever killed her husband," Maggie Lane said.

I nodded.

"I had to get out of there. I was, very simply, frightened. I'm as loyal as the next person, and I stuck with them during that awful time at the wedding. But now Mr. Bradshaw is gone. And I don't feel close enough to Heidi, and in truth, my salary is insufficient to overcome my anxiety."

"So you quit," I said.

"I resigned," she said. "Yes."

"And why was it you said that you worked for the Bradshaws plural?"

"I did," Maggie said. "I was equally assistant to both. Run the household staff, arrange their travel, see to the laundry and dry cleaning, deal with the caterer, manage their social calendar, everything . . . except finances."

"Who handled the finances?"

"Mr. Bradshaw," she said.

"Himself?" I said.

"Yes, he was very private about that."

I nodded.

"And is that what you came here to tell me?" I said. "That you worked for both of them?"

"Well, yes . . . no. I don't know. I was originally hired by Mr. Bradshaw. But what I guess I really thought you should know is that they weren't actually separated."

"Tell me about that," I said.

"He was at the island often. They were . . . When he came to the island, almost always they . . ."

Maggie's face got slightly pink. She hesitated.

"They were intimate?" I said.

"Yes," she said, "rather carelessly, I thought."

"Don't you hate that," I said. "Why the fake estrangement?"

"They never explained exactly why to me, but the official word was that she had kicked him out."

"You don't think his frequent intimate visits were an attempt to reconcile?"

"No. They explained to me carefully that they weren't really separated. But it had to do with Mr. Bradshaw's business."

"But when Bradshaw died . . ." I said.

"I felt it might be a clue," she said.

"But it wasn't a clue when Adelaide was kidnapped and six people died?"

"No, I know, it sounds foolish, but I am a loyal person."

"Is it fair to say you were more loyal to Mr. Bradshaw than to Mrs.?" I said.

"I admired him very much," she said.

"During his time there, how did he get along with his stepdaughter?"

"Oh," Maggie Lane said, "Adelaide."

"Adelaide," I said.

"It was hard to get along with Adelaide. She was so mean and whiny."

"Anger and self-pity?" I said.

"I suppose," Maggie said. "I know Mr. Bradshaw tried to befriend her. But . . ."

"Didn't like Adelaide so well yourself?"

"No. I mean, I was always thoroughly professional," Maggie said. "But she was very difficult."

"Who did Adelaide get along with?" I said.

Maggie thought for a moment, and shook her head.

"How about Maurice Lessard," I said. "Her momentary husband?"

"I really saw very little of him or of them together," Maggie said.

I nodded.

"She close to her mother?"

Maggie almost sniffed in disdain.

"Heidi never showed much mothering instinct," she said.

"How about spousal instinct?" I said.

"I saw very little," Maggie said. "It was mostly about sex and money."

"Her, too," I said.

"I think Mr. Bradshaw tried to be a good father to Adelaide and a good husband to Heidi."

"And to you?" I said.

Her face, which had gotten pinkish at the mention of intimacy between Mr. and Mrs. Bradshaw, began to glow brightly.

"He was a very kind employer," she said.

"I'm sure he was," I said. "How about intimacy?"

She didn't know what to do with her face.

"I beg your pardon?"

I smiled at her.

"Okay," I said. "I won't make you say it out loud. We both know there was intimacy. We both know you were taken with him. We both know it's why you didn't say anything until he was gone."

She put her head down into her hands.

"Don't feel bad," I said. "Most of us have thought with our pelvis at one time or another."

# 61

*We were in my office.* It was overcast outside, and raining tentatively with the promise of more vigor as the day wore on. Hawk was making coffee. I was gazing alertly out the window, assessing the rainwear of the women on the street.

"You know what I can't figure out," I said.

"Almost everything?" Hawk said.

"There's that," I said. "But more specifically, I can't figure out why women can look sexy in few clothes, and equally so in ankle-length yellow slickers."

"Maybe got to do with the woman more

than it got to do with the outfit," Hawk said.

"That's a possibility," I said.

"Or maybe it got to do with the observer," Hawk said.

"You are a deep bastard," I said.

"I am," Hawk said. "And I'm glad you focused on the big issues."

"Like why Heidi and Harden were pretending to be estranged?"

"No, I know we can't figure that out," Hawk said. "I was wondering why Bradshaw was boppin' Miss Maggie."

"Because he could?" I said.

"You and me *could*," Hawk said.

"But you and me wouldn't," I said.

"So the question remains," Hawk said.

"Supply and demand?" I said.

"Supply no issue in my life," Hawk said.

"Nor mine," I said.

"Not much variety," Hawk said. "But very high quality."

"So what else could it be," I said.

"Taste," Hawk said.

My phone rang and I answered.

"Do you know who this is?" the caller said.

Even his voice sounded gray.

"I do," I said. "Thanks for asking."

"This is the cell phone equivalent," Rugar said, "of a white flag. I am perhaps five minutes from your office. I have a young woman with me. I want no trouble."

"What do you want?"

"I want to come to your office with the young woman and talk with you."

"Hawk is here," I said.

"I assumed he would be."

"Come ahead," I said.

"No one else," Rugar said.

"Nobody but me and Hawk," I said.

"Your word," Rugar said.

"My word," I said.

"Five minutes," Rugar said.

I hung up. Hawk looked at me.

"Rugar," I said, "five minutes. Under a flag of truce. He has a young woman with him."

Hawk nodded.

"Curiouser," Hawk said, "and fucking curiouser."

# 62

*When Rugar came in,* Hawk was standing against the wall to my far left with his gun out. In honor of the truce, he let it hang at his side, pointing at the floor. I was behind my desk with my right-hand drawer open so I could reach a gun easily. Trust, but verify.

Rugar was wearing a gray trench coat and a gray snap-brim hat. With him was a young woman in jeans and a white sweater. She wore a black down vest over the sweater. Her hair was in a ponytail tucked out through the opening in an adjustable Detroit Tigers cap. She wore very little makeup. She looked to be about twenty-one.

"Adelaide?" I said.

She nodded without saying anything. I looked at Rugar.

"The truce does not extend to us letting you walk out of here with her," I said.

"She can do what she wishes," Rugar said. "I am not her captor."

He took off his trench coat and folded it neatly over the arm of Pearl's couch. He put his hat on top of it. As always, he was in gray, featuring a gray tweed jacket. His cuff links were sapphire. He took Adelaide's down vest and placed it next to his coat. Then he nodded at a chair in front of my desk. Adelaide sat in it. He turned toward Hawk.

"Hawk," he said.

Hawk nodded. Rugar sat down beside Adelaide. He looked at me.

"You're hard to kill," he said.

"So far," I said.

"You know I sent the ones who failed," he said.

"Yep," I said. "I figure you knew Leonard from Marshport, and when you wanted me aced you got hold of him, and he tried to do you a favor, which got him killed. What I don't get is why you didn't do it yourself. It's not your style to send someone."

Rugar nodded.

"I assume you killed Bradshaw," I said.

Rugar nodded.

"And now," I said, "conscience-stricken, you've come to give yourself up."

Rugar smiled faintly.

"I have a rather long story to tell you," Rugar said, "at the conclusion of which we will discuss options."

Hawk was motionless against the far wall. He could stand perfectly still for hours if there was reason to. He didn't get restless. He didn't get tired. The gun didn't get heavy. His attention didn't waver. Adelaide sat with her knees together and her hands folded in her lap. She looked different from how she had looked. Her color was better. She looked as if she might be working out. She glanced frequently at Rugar. Otherwise, she was still. I left the drawer in my desk open.

"In the early 1980s," Rugar said, "I was working for the American government in Bucharest, doing the kind of work I do."

"I know that," I said.

Rugar tipped his head forward a little.

"I've never doubted that you're smart," Rugar said.

"Industrious," I said.

Rugar smiled again without any humor.

"Both," he said. "During that period I ran across an American named Harden Bradshaw. He was working for the embassy in some sort of propaganda capacity, and having an affair with a woman named Heidi Van Meer, who'd followed him to Romania, though she was still married to Peter Van Meer and remained so for six more years."

I nodded.

"You knew that?" Rugar said.

I nodded again.

"You are industrious," he said. "During the time when she was in Bucharest with Bradshaw, I met Heidi, and we had a brief sexual relationship."

"Excuse me, Adelaide, but Heidi has probably had a sexual relationship with Namu the killer whale," I said.

This time Rugar's smile hinted at actual amusement.

"I was hoping that she might be more selective, but I don't think the exaggeration is misplaced."

"I think it was sort of how she got to be Heidi," I said.

Rugar nodded.

"Have I told you anything new?" he said.

"I figured you knew Bradshaw and probably Heidi. It was too big a coincidence that you and she and her third husband were all in Bucharest at the same time and twentysomething years later you appear and shoot up a wedding."

"That was not quite the plan," Rugar said. "But I don't want to get ahead of myself."

"No rush," I said.

Adelaide kept a check on Rugar as the story spooled out, but more and more she was watching me, too.

"We did not have a very long run, Heidi and I," Rugar said. "My income fluctuates. But it never constituted great wealth. Heidi was adroit and very much enjoyed physical sensation. I don't believe she ever felt very much else."

I looked at Adelaide.

"Do you mind hearing this about your mother?" I said.

"No," Adelaide said.

I looked back at Rugar.

"I left Bucharest at the end of 1984," Rugar said. "And went on to Berlin and elsewhere. Heidi returned to her husband, Peter Van Meer. Adelaide was born in 1985. Heidi continued her affair with Bradshaw while living with Van Meer until 1990, when she divorced Van Meer, whose wealth had begun to decline, and married Bradshaw, whose wealth had increased dramatically with the death of his father."

"What's love got to do with it?" I said.

"Somewhere in the year 2004, Bradshaw's wealth began to decline. He would never be poor in terms we would understand," Rugar said. "But in a few years he would be unable to maintain Heidi at the level of exorbitance that she required."

"And she came to you," I said.

"They did, a few months ago," Rugar said. "In Bucharest all those years ago, Bradshaw had become fascinated with the kind of specialty service I was able to perform. If he ever needed such, he asked, how could he reach me? I provided him a means."

"Both of them," I said.

"So Maggie Lane was right," I said. "The estrangement was pretense."

Rugar smiled.

"You underestimate Heidi," he said. "It was, and was not, a pretense. She separated from him to coerce him but gave him sexual access, to keep him tied to her."

I glanced at Adelaide. She was nodding slowly.

"Was Bradshaw in on it all the way?" I said.

"No, he was the yenta," Rugar said. "Once he had reconnected us, he stepped away. I think he felt that the less he knew, the less he could be asked if things went badly."

"So it was you and she?" I said.

"Yes."

"From my vantage point," I said, "it is the most cockamamie scheme I've ever seen. What were you thinking?"

"Adelaide was engaged to be married to Maurice Lessard, whose family had more money than they could ever run out of. Adelaide would be his heir, from the moment of *I do*. Heidi was very careful about that. Bradshaw's major asset was his large insurance policy in Heidi's benefit, which he still maintained through the separation."

"Which was probably another reason for

her to remain in"—I glanced at Adelaide— "ah, sexual proximity."

"Surely," Rugar said. "Heidi's plan was as follows. At the wedding, as soon as the vows were sealed, I would kidnap Adelaide. In the process I would kill Maurice Lessard, and Bradshaw. I would hold Adelaide for ransom, which Heidi felt sure her new in-laws would pay. She would collect on the insurance, get the ransom, be reunited with her daughter, and then Heidi and I could be together again with more money than we would ever need, especially when Adelaide shared her inheritance from Maurice. The whole thing would be done in such a way as to take the focus off the two murders."

"Which," I said, "if they were just routine murders, the cops would look at once for who benefited. And the finger of suspicion would point at Heidi and Adelaide."

"Exactly," Rugar said.

"But if they seemed an accidental by-product of a kidnapping attempt . . ."

"They would expend most of their energy looking for Adelaide."

"And you'd get to walk into the sunset with Heidi," I said.

Rugar's smile was cold.

"I knew better," he said.

"But you went for it?"

"I rejected it. I told her the plan was too convoluted. That she'd have to find some-one else. I didn't bother to ask her how her daughter might feel."

"She said no, it had to be me. She couldn't trust anyone else to do it."

"I thanked her for her confidence but declined. And she said, 'All right. I wasn't going to tell you, but I have no choice.' I said it won't make any difference what you tell me. And she said, 'Adelaide is your daughter.'"

# 63

*It was perhaps the longest silence* I've ever sat through. Nobody spoke. Nobody moved. Except that Hawk tapped his gun slowly against his thigh as he stood. Behind me, through my bay windows, the day was darker, and the rain was hard now, streaming down the glass. Finally, Rugar spoke.

"I was somewhat startled myself," he said.

"Have you authenticated the relationship?" I said.

"DNA," Rugar said. "She is my daughter."

"Did you know, Adelaide?"

"Not until my mother told us," she said. "And even then I didn't believe it until we had the DNA test. It made it easier to go through the kidnapping."

I nodded.

"And that's why you did it?" I said to Rugar.

"Yes," he said. "I have no relatives. The thought of having one pleased me."

"I'm surprised," I said.

"As am I," Rugar said.

"Until now you had thought Van Meer was your father," I said to Adelaide.

"Yes."

"Were you close to him?"

"No," she said.

"How do you feel about your new father?" I said.

"I love him," she said. "Papa is the first person I've ever had."

I looked at Hawk. Silently, he mouthed the word *Papa*.

I looked at Rugar. He nodded.

"Okay, Papa," I said. "Then what happened."

"I knew enough about Heidi to know she would find someone to do this foolish scheme if I declined," Rugar said. "And at least if I did it, I could see that it was done well, and I could look out for Adelaide."

"So you agreed."

"I told her I would do it," Rugar said. "But she was to do nothing without clearing it with me."

"Which she agreed to and ignored," I said.

"She hired you," Rugar said. "That would have been a dealbreaker had I known in advance."

"Why'd she do it?" I said.

"Probably because I frightened her, and the entire adventure frightened her, and she wanted personal protection from someone who knew me."

"She had the Tashtego patrol," I said.

"She knew that those on duty would have to be eliminated if this scheme were to work."

"So she hired me to protect her from the consequences of an action she initiated," I said.

"Yes."

"That's crazy," I said.

"I have thought since the beginning that some of what we were doing is putting on a kidnapping that was worthy of Heidi Bradshaw, and I still think so."

I nodded.

"But hiring you was the ultimate mistake," Rugar said. "I knew you would not leave it alone. I should have killed you as soon as I saw you."

"Yeah," I said. "You should have."

"It would have jeopardized the timetable. And it would have caused several formidable people, on both sides of the law, to attempt revenge."

Softly from his place at the wall, Hawk said, "Uh-huh."

"Later," Rugar said, "I tried to rectify my mistake by making another one. If you were to be killed, I should have done it myself."

"But," I said, "you had Adelaide to think about. You couldn't take the same risks you would once have taken."

"Your mind is quick," he said. "What has made me so successful in my profession is that I am not bothered by death, and until Adelaide, that included my own."

"Things do change," I said.

"They do," Rugar said.

"Things went awry, too," I said.

"Yes," Rugar said. "As you know, I am meticulous. But the plan was too foolish, and my co-conspirators were too . . ."

"Crazy," I said.

"Something like that."

"Was Bradshaw in on any of this?"

"I think," Rugar said, "that he thought he was."

He smiled faintly. "I doubt that he was apprised that I was to kill him."

"He didn't show," I said.

"No."

"And the hurricane was hard to plan for."

"It was. Obviously, when Bradshaw didn't show up, and the hurricane did," Rugar said, "I began to improvise. And you know how that went. I got as much done as I could, and I got Adelaide and myself out of there."

"You could still have pulled off most of it," I said. "Maybe all of it, you ended up killing Bradshaw anyway."

"I took Adelaide to a safe house and had a doctor in to see her," Rugar said. "I have, as you might imagine, considerable access to covert amenities."

"When she fainted," I said, "it was real."

Rugar looked at Adelaide.

"Yes," she said. "I didn't realize how violent it all was going to be. Momma never said anything about Maurice being killed."

"You loved Maurice?" I said.

"Not like a husband, but like a friend, yes."

"Maurice was gay," I said.

"Yes. Marriage was Mother's idea."

"You didn't mind marrying a gay man?"

She shrugged. "At least he was nice," she said.

"And you're still in the safe house?" I said.

Rugar smiled and didn't answer. I nodded.

"So you hid out in the safe house," I said, "and while you were doing it you got to know each other."

"Yes."

"And you found out some things," I said.

"Yes."

"Like that she had attempted suicide," I said.

Rugar nodded.

"And that she had been sexually molested," I said.

"Bradshaw," Rugar said. "For years."

"Did you tell anyone?" I said to Adelaide.

"Momma knew."

"What did she say?"

"She said I'd have to put up with it, for a while at least, because we didn't have any money."

Again, silence. I think even Hawk was appalled. He had stopped slapping the gun against his thigh. The only sound in the room was the rain on the window. Adelaide started to cry. I gave her a Kleenex. Rugar put his hand on her back.

"Which," I said, "finally is why you killed Bradshaw. It had nothing to do with insurance."

"Correct," Rugar said.

"And why you never sent a ransom note, which eventually forced Heidi to make a very late and amateurish forgery."

"Correct."

"You were supposed to get, what, the ransom money?"

"Yes."

"And you walked away from it?" I said.

"I didn't want it," Rugar said. "Adelaide didn't want her inheritance."

"So why didn't you just take her and go?" I said.

"You," Rugar said. "I knew you would not let it go. If you thought there was a possibility that the young girl, whom you perceived a kidnap victim, were still alive, you'd plow along looking for her. We could never be safe."

"Bradshaw called me a little while before he died and said he was in danger," I said.

"I wanted him to feel fear, as Adelaide had. I couldn't afford to let it linger as long as it should have. But I told him I would kill him and I gave him a little time to be terrified before I killed him."

"And you weren't worried about Adelaide."

"Adelaide is getting help, she is becoming more stable . . . and"—Rugar smiled—"killing Bradshaw was a somewhat smaller challenge than killing you."

"Heidi called on me for help as well," I said.

"I told her I knew everything about Adelaide and Bradshaw and her."

"So she's afraid you'll kill her," I said.

"Adelaide has asked me not to," Rugar said.

I nodded.

"Have we left anything out?" I said.

"Probably," Rugar said. "But you have most of it."

"Enough," I said.

"Except," Rugar said.

"Except," I said.

Another faint smile from Rugar. He might have humanized slightly, but he hadn't become snuggly.

"Except where do we go from here?" Rugar said.

"Exactly," I said.

# 64

It was very dark outside, though it was early in the day. And the rain was falling hard. It was so dense on my windows that the view was distorted.

"Adelaide," I said. "Tell me about . . . Papa."

"I don't know very much about him," she said with very little affect in her voice. "But I love him and he loves me. Neither of us has anyone else in the world. We have found each other."

I looked at Rugar.

"How many people you kill in this deal?" I said.

Rugar thought a minute.

"Two at the altar," he said. "Four security people, would be six. If you count Bradshaw, seven."

"And some other people died because of it," I said.

"Um-hm."

"You see my problem," I said.

"Yes," Rugar said. "And you see mine. If you continue to pursue this, what will become of Adelaide, if you should prevail."

I nodded.

"The man you thought was your father?" I said. "Van Meer? Could you find any solace with him?"

"He's an empty drunk," Adelaide said flatly. "He says things but does nothing."

"So he's not much of an option."

"None," she said.

There was something about the affectless little voice that made what she said seem absolute.

"Hard question, Adelaide, but . . . what happens if you lose Papa?"

"I will die," she said.

I looked at Rugar. His face showed nothing. I looked at Hawk. His face showed the same thing.

"You got a plan?" I said to Rugar.

"Adelaide has been mistreated all her life," he said. "She and I will go away and allow her to heal. You will never see either of us again."

"And a bunch of people died for nothing?"

"Destroying Adelaide's life will not bring them back."

"And Heidi?" I said. "We leave Heidi in place?"

"You do with Heidi what you will," Rugar said. "You are resourceful; perhaps knowing what you know, you can make a case against her without us."

I sat back and tilted my chair and looked at them. Then I leaned forward and closed the gun drawer, and stood and turned my back on them and stared through the rain-shimmered window out at the dark streets. Most of the cars had their headlights on. The wipers struggled with the rain. Then I turned back. Hawk had put his gun away, though he still stood by the wall. I took in some air and let it out and walked to the file cabinet where the coffeemaker sat. I opened the bottom drawer and took out a bottle of Bushmills Irish whiskey, and four of the little transparent plastic cups that always horrified Susan when I used them. I poured an inch of whiskey into each and handed out the cups.

Everyone stared at me.

I raised my cup.

"One for the road," I said.

Adelaide looked quickly at Rugar. Rugar smiled at her.

"He has taken our deal," Rugar said.

We drank. Adelaide handled the straight booze as well as anyone. Then Rugar stood. Adelaide stood up with him.

"We will never be friends," Rugar said. "But we will never again be enemies."

I nodded. Rugar glanced at Hawk and nodded once. Hawk nodded back. Then Rugar and Adelaide left. I sat back down behind my desk and poured another drink. Hawk sat down on the other side of my desk and held out his cup and I poured him some.

"You let him go," Hawk said.

I nodded.

"Soft as mush," Hawk said.

I nodded.

We drank our whiskey.

"Had him right here," Hawk said. "Between us. Had a confession, witnessed by me. And you let him go."

I nodded. We drank some more whiskey. The rain hammered down in the near darkness.

"You think you can get Heidi without him?"

"Gonna try," I said.

"Ten times the work it woulda been, you hadn't let him go."

I nodded. We hadn't turned the lights on in my office. We sat in semidarkness drinking straight whiskey.

"What would you have done?" I said after a while.

"Let him go," Hawk said.

His face was without expression.